Jessie Margaret Edmondston Saxby

Lichens from the Old Rock

Poems

Jessie Margaret Edmondston Saxby

Lichens from the Old Rock
Poems

ISBN/EAN: 9783337401528

Printed in Europe, USA, Canada, Australia, Japan

Cover: Foto ©Andreas Hilbeck / pixelio.de

More available books at **www.hansebooks.com**

LICHENS FROM THE OLD ROCK

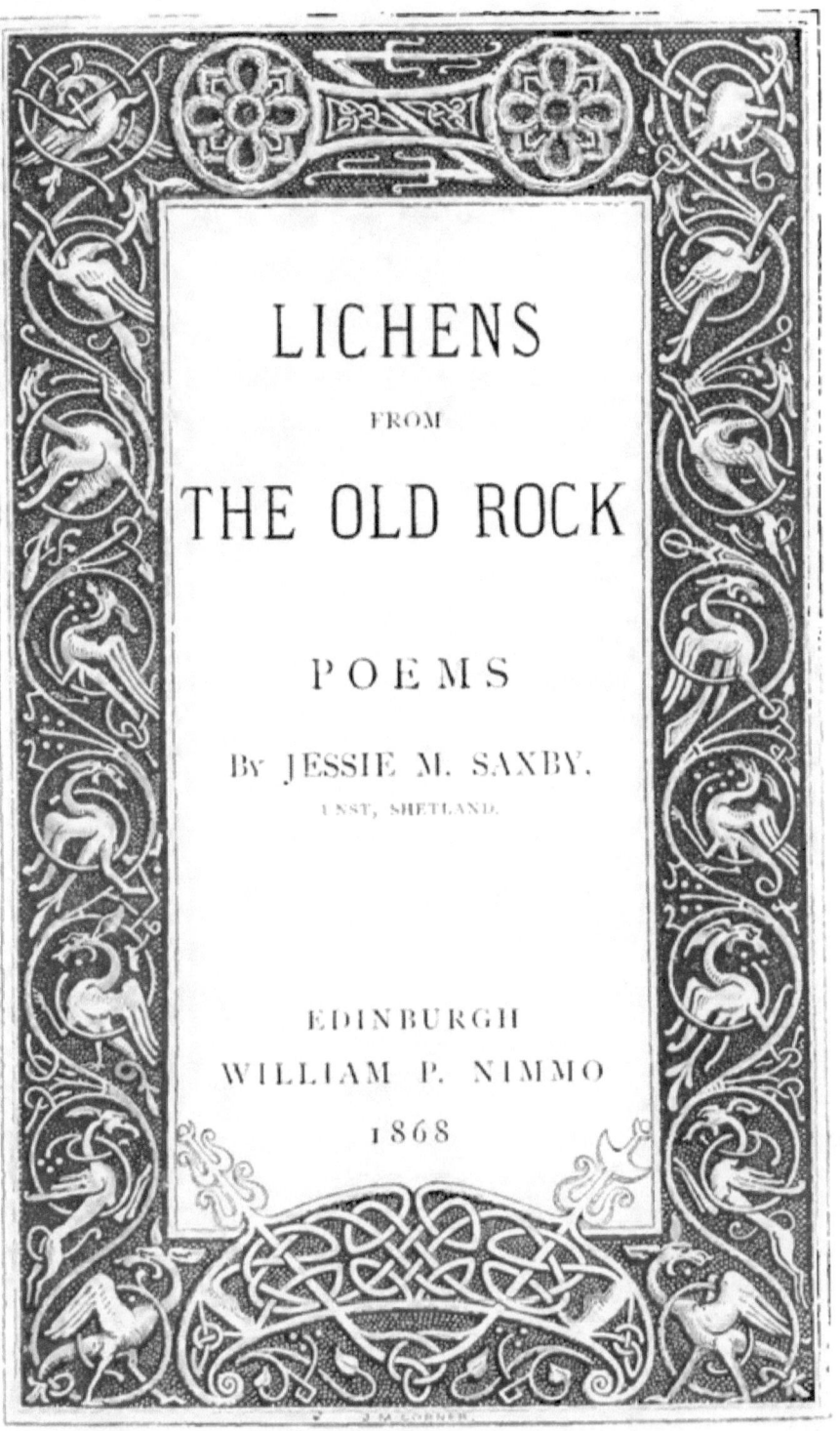

LICHENS

FROM

THE OLD ROCK

POEMS

By JESSIE M. SAXBY.

UNST, SHETLAND.

EDINBURGH

WILLIAM P. NIMMO

1868

TO

SHETLAND AND THE SHETLANDERS

THIS LITTLE VOLUME

IS

AFFECTIONATELY DEDICATED

BY

THE AUTHOR.

PREFACE.

✦

IT is certain that many of my fellow-countrymen, who
are now toiling in distant lands, occasionally derive no
small amount of pleasure from the mere contemplation
of a tiny flower, a withered sprig of heath, or even
a rude unshapely fragment of lichen, which, in days
gone by, has been gathered by a friendly hand from
their native rocks. To those individuals themselves,
and also to those of my readers who can appreciate
the mind which does not estimate such humble me-
mentoes according to their intrinsic worth, I chiefly
look for indulgence, trusting that my object in offering this little collection of poems, may be deemed at
least a small compensation for the numerous errors
and shortcomings, which so inevitably accompany
want of experience.

BALTASOUND, SHETLAND ISLES,
February 1868.

CONTENTS.

CONTENTS.

CONTENTS.

LICHENS FROM THE OLD ROCK.

I STOOD beside the frowning crags one even,
And gazing up into the dim blue heaven,
Methought a shadowy spirit floated by
And rested on the water heaving nigh ;
And then, as still I gazed, its cold thin hand
Was stretched towards me with a waving wand :
Then straight my spirit sank away in sleep,
And visions strange rose from the billowy deep,
Gathering around my sadly-troubled brain,
And guiding thought with wild uncertain rein.
It seemed as if I lived in ages past,
Ere Time had swept o'er earth like some rude blast.
And gazing on my country's rugged face
I sought in vain for some soft verdant trace
Of Nature's loving hand.   But naught was there.
Save giant cliffs, whose beetled brows were bare
And grim and gaunt.
                    But ere my voice could call
For floral gifts upon my land to fall,
Methought the Spirit of the Water said—

" Behold thine ancient rocks that I have made
So bare and chill, so rude, so grand, so wild ;
There rests not on their foreheads one fair child
To clothe, with flowery grace, each sterile brow
That rises bare to meet the cloudlets now ;
My wet and glittering wreath of crested foam
Alone adorns each dark and lofty dome."
The Spirit ceased, and straight there seemed to rise
From every tuft of grass a world of sighs.
And while the crags e'en frowned there fluttered forth
From every furrow Spirits of the North.
With angry eyes that spake unfathomed woe.
Around those rocks they wandered to and fro ;
Where'er they lit they left a verdant trace,
Nor ceased until each worn and rugged face
Was garlanded anew.   Where ferns or flowers
Could find no safety from the drenching showers.
There hung they brilliant lichens, and the sun
Bade radiant hues dwell on them.

It was done,
The Spirits' tender task, and back they fled,
Each to his tuft of grass or stony bed.
And then the vision changed, and still in dreams
I seemed to stand below the evening beams.
Gazing upon the flood.—But full of years,
And bowed by times of toil and falling tears.

Yet clinging to my old gray islands still
With love that care and sorrow could not kill.
Methought I saw with joy that time had fanned
Into full day the gifts that Spirit band
Had once conferred, and everywhere around
The crags with rainbow-coloured hues were crowned.
Then spake the Water Spirit once again :
" Let not their loving purposes be vain ;
Go gather from thy rocks such fragments rare
As come within thy grasp, with heedful care
Preserve thou them.   Let higher hearts than thine
Find jewels to set, and flowers to sweetly twine.
But be thy work the *humble* patriot's task
To find the modest gifts that lowliest bask
Upon thy country's brow,—'tis all they ask.
And 'twill repay thee well ; for little things
Do ofttimes rise upon the lightest wings.
And should none other bless thy loving hand.
The Spirit-forms that guard thy native land
Will give thee Spirit-thanks for having found
The loved though lowly gifts they shed around."

THE SIGNAL FIRES.

TOWARDS the northern extremity of this island (Unst) is a pretty little bay which bears the name of Haroldswick, and at the foot of one of the hills which surround the valley is a quaint old heap of stones known to every Shetlander as "Harold's Grave."

In the days of yore, when might made right, and poor Hialtland was continually harassed by invading foemen—Vikings like themselves—it was the custom, if a hostile sail was seen to approach the land, for those who observed it to light signal fires on their hill-tops, as a warning to the neighbouring islands.

On the evening of our Prince's wedding-day, the kindly Shetlanders rose up from their firesides, where, perchance, they had been listening to tales of the ancient time, and with joyous loyalty lighted bonfires on all the principal hills throughout their islands. Never on these mountain-peaks had fires been lit since the days when the proud old flag of Denmark had waved in the ocean breeze, and claimed for the Danish crown the fealty of the islanders. And very brightly blazed the fires in rejoicing for an English Edward's marriage, and in welcoming a Danish princess to reign once more over Shetland hearts.

The following poem was suggested by some of the incidents before mentioned.

THE dreamy, distant, polar star,
Looked from his icy home afar,
    On Thule's "classic land."
He saw King Harold's ships of war
Riding within the tidal bar,
    His Vikings on the strand.

Their banners streamed all wild and gay,
Their armour glistened with the spray,
    Their haughty hearts heaved high.
Proud looked the Norse sea-king that day
He landed by the crescent bay.
    He came to win or die.

Upon each mountain's rugged height
Gleamed luridly the watch-fire's light—
    Isle signalled unto isle
That each should send its men of might,
That each should join in desperate fight,
    Where Harold waits the while.

And Hialtland's sons were dauntless men,
They knew no fear, no equal then,
    In those grand days of yore.
Fate's page was sealed for Harold when
He fought that battle nigh the fen
    That skirts our northern shore.

Strong hands that day to death were wed,
Brave were the many hearts that bled,
    And Harold's high soul burned :
For of the warrior band he led,
The boldest, best, were with the dead,
The rest had yielded or had fled,
    And such a fate *he* spurned.

He gazed upon the island foe,
And then upon his dead below,
    And then upon the sky,
Where saw he bright Aurora glow,
And flit like phantoms to and fro,
Or like the shades of those who go
    To Odin's halls on high.

The hill was echoing back the yell
Of triumph,—on his ear it fell
    As blight on blooming flower—
His foemen's shout, his dying knell,
And Harold breathed a mute farewell
    As dawned the morning hour.

The conquerors laid their weapons by,
And when the sun rose in the sky
    They bade the flames expire.

When night came next it wrapped the shore
In misty veil—and never more
    Was waked that warning fire.

———

The dreamy, distant, polar star,
Looks from his icy home afar.
    On Thule's " classic land ;"
On mountains in each grey-clad isle
Is raised a gleaming fiery pile,
    Lit by an eager band.

King Harold and his Vikings brave
Each rest within a rocky grave,
    In shadow of the hill ;
The fires that glow on mountain-brow
Are lit in hope and gladness now,
    Nor thought is there of ill.

One comes from yonder northern shore,
And as Norse Harold did of yore
    For conquest does she come.
He brought a tyrant's iron glove,
She comes unarm'd by all save love.
    Oh ! bid her welcome home.

Our fathers lit the wild watch-fires,
And we will do as did our sires,
  But not for warning dread;
They woke those flames in wroth and fear.
We wake them that the world may hear
  We joy our Prince will wed
A daughter of the old Norse kings,
Who comes on love's own golden wings,
  In love's own fetters led.

We light the fires, and pray that she
May to our glorious nation be
  A joy, a hope, a pride.
God save the heir of England's crown,
And shed the choicest blessings down
  Upon his Norland bride !

SHETLAND'S OFFERING TO THE PRINCESS.

DAUGHTERS of Shetland! unite heart and hand,
Weave magic mantles, the best of your land ;
No finger will weary that hovers above
Needles that frame such an offering of love.
  For the Flower of Denmark's line,
  For the blooming " laughing vine,"
  Whose young hands have come to grasp
  England's oak with loving clasp ;
  For the Princess whose fair feet
  Stand on Albion's proudest seat ;
  For the Bride whose maidenhood
  Pattern was of all things good ;
  For the Wife. so young and fair,
  Who will teach us virtues rare :
  For the Gem our Prince hath set
  In his royal coronet ;
  For the Star whose brilliant light
  Came to make a sad home bright ;
  For the Joy of hearts that grieve.
  Shetland maidens, offerings weave :

Take the gift, Princess, from isles of the sea,
Daughters of Vikinger send it to thee ;
Take, too, the blessing each heart poureth forth,
Hearts loyal and true to thee, Star of the North!

A VOICE FROM SHETLAND.

October 1864.

THE winter wi' its creepin' cauld is noo no far awa',
Its days o' dreary darkness, and its lang, lang, nichts
o' snaw;
And my puir wee bits o' bairnies can neither rin or
play,
For cotton frocks are unco thin wi' sic a bitter day.

They're sittin' coorin' round the fire, and ilka little
thing
Is wonderin' when its faither comes what he may
chance ta bring.
Oh, weel they ken if he's no back before it's time for
bed,
They'll hae nae " afternuin " this nicht, for *I* hae nae
bit bread.

I wish they a' were gaen ta sleep, for oh, wae, wae, is
me!
I saw their faither's boat come hame lang syne afae
the sea,

I saw him gang atae the yaird wi' weary waesome face ;
He couldna bear ta meet his bairns' eager quest'nin'
    gaze.

His keshie hung across his arm, I ken nae fish was
    there ;
And this is how he's aye come back ; ay, but my heart
    is sair.
This simmer's been a woefu' time, no ae fish ta be
    got,
And noo the winter's comin' nigh, and hard will be
    our lot.

Nae oil ta licht the lingering nichts, and mak them
    spin awa' ;
Nae claes ta clad our bairns in, ta keep them frae the
    snaw ;
Nae food ta fill the peerie mou's, ta roond ilk little
    limb ;
Nae extra pence ta keep the hoose. fu' lichtsome, trig.
    and trim.

And I am no the only ane ta mak this waesome
    plaint—
There's mony a fisher's wife 'ill feel her mither heart
    gae faint,

As lookin' on her hungry babes, she'll mind the
    winter's nigh,
And simmer's fishin' season *gaen*, and no ae grot
    laid by.

Oh wae is me! oh wae is me! nae wonder that I
    greet,
But Magnie mustna see me sae, he has eneugh ta
    meet ;
Eneugh o' sorrow he will spy in ilka bairnie's ee—
His little anes, whose lives depend on what he wins
    at sea.

There's just ae comfort that I hae. and it maks up
    for a'.
Our Heavenly Faither kens our wants, He sees us,
    great and sma',
He loes the peerie bairnies weel. *He'll* keep them
    frae the cauld ;
And if they canna stay wi' us, He'll tak' them tae
    His fauld.

THE SPIRIT BAND.*

THE night was still, expectant, dark, and dense.
The queenly moon had left her cloudy throne,
And stars had all withdrawn their modest eyes
From Nature's drowsy face of sombre care.
I looked up at the deep blue vault of Heaven—
Not even flecked by one soft snowy cloud—
And saw a silent host of spirits fair
Glide fitfully along the solemn sky,
Filling its trembling air with life and light.
They numbered few, but as the moments sped
The phantom band increased. They ranged themselves
In one great gleaming rainbow-shaped device,
A little way above the mountain's top ;
And then their tempered armour glistened with
A thousand shades of softly blended hues.
Their radiant eyes gave forth the light of stars.
Up—shooting up—into the wide expanse

* The Spirit Band—the Aurora Borealis ; poetically sup-
posed to be the spirits of the ancient Vikings.

Of Heaven's lone, azure, night-bound fields
Those wondrous revellers glide.
                  They had come forth
From Odin's mystic cave to gaze upon
The land they loved and had inhabited.
Once—long ago—they roamed from spot to spot
As conquerors and heroes—hated, feared.
Lords of the ocean, they had gloried in
The name of Viking in those brave old days.
A time *had been* when mountain, forest, isle,
Had humbly owned their mighty master sway.
But all that wild romance is over now,
And Viking deeds live but in Scaldic rhyme.
The stalwart forms that once had braved alike
The hurricanes of war, of wold, of wave,
Had even ceased to be the ocean's toys,
And age on age has been since they have lived.
Their recreant sons have half-forgot the name—
The glorious name—borne by their sires of old,
Whose warrior-spirits in Valhalla's halls
Now sadly drain the sacred bowl, nor care
To fill it up anew to the old pledge—
The patriot pledge—of " Skoal to Northland, skoal."
But hark ! what loud-voiced thunder-cloud has borne
To the All-Father's festive board the tale
Of a bright northern star in the ascendant !

Hark ! how the grey-beards of Valhalla chant
Their fierce triumphant songs of joy for her,
The daughter of their line, who stands before
The wondering world, while o'er her beauteous brow
Earth's proudest diadem is hovering.
Hark ! how they drain the skull-cup once again.
When to their ears is borne the soldier shout
Proclaiming ancient Denmark's modern might—
Might that dare cope with tenfold deadly odds.
Then issuing in a ghostly train—those shades
Of the old pirate kings bound swiftly up
Towards the brooding sky, while from their path
The placid queen of night departs in haste ;
They bid the quivering stars to droop their lids
Before the majesty of spirit-light.
Behold them clad in glittering festal robes,
Their garments floating in the evening air.
And wildly gleaming through the wakened clouds.
Like nothing born of sea or land.
                              They pause.
And poise in silence for one moment's space.
They see a royal infant cradled on
A young, sweet mother's doating heart.   They see
Him girt about by a great nation's prayers.
They gaze upon this child of many hopes,
And their pale shadowy forms dilate with pride

For on his baby-features the boy bears
The impress of his northern ancestors.
" Our name, our great world-wide earn'd name.
Will live again," these old sea-kings exclaim.
" The rays from our immortal forms of light
Will ne'er be needed *now* to chase the night
From Norland skies ; for Norland's noblest star
Has pierced the gloom of many a cloudy bar ;
And Norland's ancient fame and ancient glory
Are blended now with England's mighty story."
The phantom-band then bent their shining wings,
And the low quiver of their raiment fell
Upon my ear as echoing sounds that dwell
(After some heavenly strain) among harp-strings.
All silently and swiftly, one by one,
That train of " northern lights " grew distant, dim.
At last, Heaven's face was once more sad and lone.
And brooding night crept to the horizon's rim.
Then evening wrapped her dense and dismal veil
Still closer round the earth and ocean pale ;
And the pole-star rose above the shadowy hill,
The only gem that decked that midnight still.

THE MARGARITA* TO THE CONCHOLOGIST.

OH ! lay for one moment your lens aside,
And close down the volume so deep and wide.
I, your Margarita, am fain to tell
The legends that live in my fairy shell.

I've come from the depths where the ocean laves
The caverns wild that are Vikings' graves;
I've come from the plains 'neath the angry brine,
Where mermaiden grottoes of ivory fine
Are decked with the sea-plants and coralline.

I've come from the tomb of the sailor boy
Whose barklet was crushed like a fragile toy ;
She lies meekly there with her brave young dead,
And the rude surf champs o'er her watery bed.

* The Margarita, a rare shell lately discovered in the Shetland seas, by a well-known conchologist.

I've come from the wave-washed fields far down.
'Neath the proud sea's crested and white-tipped crown.
Where delicate flowers of the ocean born
Weep pale for their parents' destructive scorn.

I have come to tell to your trancéd ear,
Of beautiful things that you see not here,
Of gems of a loveliness matchless fair,
Of shells that you call far more bright and rare.

Ah yes ! for what is a shapeless stone,
Though it gleam like a midnight star alone ?
And what are the pearls that the shell-fish wear,
Can they with *us* in our beauty compare ?

You have marked how faultless our well-curved forms.
They were never made for a life of storms,
But to live like sunbeams or drops of dew.
And tenderly cared by the " favoured few."

Then cherish us well, you have ta'en us away
From the home we loved 'neath the glistening spray.
And sometimes list to the silvery bell
That whispers you low from the " rose-lipped shell."

THE SEA STORM.

WINDS are raging fierce and high,
Lurid lightnings wreathe the sky,
Thunders roll and night is nigh,
Ships 'mid storm-toss'd breakers lie
            At the ocean's will.
Little ones there are who weep,
Wives who weary vigils keep,
When all else have gone to sleep.
Father! to yon angry deep
            Say Thou, " Peace, be still."

Wildly heaves the troubled wave
Round the bark that bears the brave ;
Far and lone those waters rave,
None are nigh to help or save.
            And in some far home,
Sheltered from the storm, there be
Hearts whose every thought will flee
To the loved *this* night at sea.
Father! all their hope's in Thee,
            Guard those on the foam.

By our crag-bound northern shore.
Rocks a ship with goodly store ;
Will she ride these breakers o'er !
Will she gain her port once more ?
    Will the rude sea spare !
In a sunny Indian land,
Mourns a heavy-hearted band :
By yon bleak and surly strand,
On a bed of shifting sand,
    Lies a vessel fair.

Cradled by the restless tide
Sleep the manly loved, the pride
Of the eyes that weep beside
Southern streams. The deep defied
    Boasted human power.
But though none were nigh to tell,
None to hear the doomed ones' knell,
God was there. His whispers fell
On their ears, and all was well,
    Even in such an hour.

Where the wide Atlantic boils
Like a cauldron, vainly toils
A lone ship ; from various soils
Came her pirate crew and spoils.
    Ha ! a flash of light.

From a thunder-cloud's dark crown,
Strikes the hull—hoarse breezes drown
Prayers and curses, heaven doth frown,
And the ravening sea sucks down
        Prey she deems her right.

On a mountain-billow's crest
Lies a barklet sore distrest,
And as bird when it would rest
Folds its wings on ocean's breast.
        Strikes she now her sail.
And against the warring sky
Rise her frail spars bared and high ;
Upward turns each sailor eye,
For they know that One is nigh
        Who will hear their wail.

Far from land, 'mid gloom and night,
Oh, 'tis vain to strive, to fight,
'Gainst the storm-king in his might.
Father ! guide their skiff aright,
        Stretch o'er her Thy hand.
From the lighthouse-lamp are borne
Rays to guide the tempest-torn ;
Soon will dawn the cheerful morn.
Father ! comfort hearts forlorn,
        Bring them safe to land.

Hark ! amidst the tempest's gloom
Comes a deep and solemn boom ;
'Tis a signal from some bark
Struggling blindly in the dark
   'Gainst the wind and wave.
Oft that crew had braved the gale,
Oft unfurled a tattered sail,
Laughed to hear the mad winds rail,
Hearkened to the drowning wail—
   Sailors true and brave.

Will they weather out this storm ?
Will each stalwart trusty form
Reach the calm still haven nigh ?
Father ! keep them 'neath Thine eye,
   Hear the whispered prayer :
Bid the ocean cease its strife,
Calm the fears of child and wife,
Bid the angry winds be still,
Let the sailor know no ill
   While within Thy care.

THE SHETLAND FOWLER.

THE rocks are rugged, forbidding, and bare,
And none but the fowler may venture there;
But sorrow and want are the shades that brood
O'er the home where his children cry for food.

To nature he turns—he is nature's child,
And will dare to invade those grey cliffs wild,
He will dare to climb to the sea-birds' nest,
Where he'll pluck the down from the brooding breast,
To warm the nestlings *he* loves the best.

He scans each crag with an eager eye,
Above is the blue of a summer sky,
Beneath rolls the ocean whose foamy crest
Showers spray on the cliff by the eagle's nest.

And the red flush mounts to the fowler's brow,
He has found what he vainly sought till now.
The eyry of eagles. No thought he hath
Of the death that lurks by the rocky path.

With a dauntless mien, but a cautious tread.
He mounts the rude rockway without a dread ;
No foot, save of wild bird, hath rested there,
He goes where the boldest could never dare.

The eagle soars from his home to the sky,
And loudly screams his defiant cry ;
For the spoiler hath breathlessly paused to rest,
Where lingers the mate on the ancient nest.

The man stands alone on that dizzy height,
And the bird lies vanquished by human might.
'Twas a dauntless feat, and 'twas bravely done ;
He dared all danger—he dared and won.

HASCOSS OF NORWAY.

FROM Norwegian stormy mountains
   Came a lonely stranger here,
Claiming from his brother Norsemen,
   Welcome, shelter, home, and cheer.

Gloom was on his careworn forehead,
   Sorrow lurked within his eye,
Breaking heart and bruiséd spirit
   Sent their echoes in his sigh.

Silent, weary, was the wanderer,
   Coldly shunning scenes of glee,
Brooding o'er some secret suffering,
   Gazing sadly on the sea.

To his side there came a maiden,
   In her eye a dancing light,
Springing step, and golden tresses
   Shining like the moon at night.

Rapt she gazed upon the mourner,
   Old Norwegian lays sang he,

Never had her glad ear hearkened
  To such plaintive melody.

All the anguish seething in him,
  All the tears he might have wept,
Flowed in melancholy wailings
  From the chords his fingers swept.

And the warblings of his violin
  Took from grief its keenest sting :
Sole memorial of his country
  Was this loved and lifeless thing—
Voices speaking to his memory,
  Seemed each sweet-toned murmuring string.

Oft the maiden came and listened
  To that music wild and rare,
Only in her gentle glances
  Sympathising with his care.

Ne'er a word her sweet lips uttered,
  Ne'er a thought or hope breathed he,
Only with his lays he wooed her,
  Only with her eyes spake she.

Thus she won him from his sorrows,
  Thus *he* won her kindly heart,
And no more to wild Norwegia
  Did the stranger's feet depart.

WE knew not, we knew not, how perished those
    men,
Who left us to dream of a meeting again.
They launched out their bark on the treacherous foam
And never came back to their own island home.

A widow's lone hope and a young maiden's pride,
A sister's kind brother, the loved of a bride,
A father of infants, a mother's delight,
All sank 'neath the waves on that terrible night.

Our Hialtland was gladdened by sunbeams that day.
They left it with hearts brimming happy and gay ;
But the wings of the night brought to ocean a gale.
And they struck to its fury their barklet's bright sail.

We knew not, we knew not, how perished those men,
The brave hearts we loved, and that came not again ;
Oh ! we only could know that with land on their lea,
And their homesteads in sight, they went down 'neath
    the sea.

Did they weep that so soon they were hurried away?
Did they rave in their terror, or silently pray?
Did they conquer each feeling of love or of hate?
Did they sternly and manfully turn to their fate?

Did some merciless billow sweep over their path,
And shatter their skiff in a moment of wrath?
Or with strong hearts undaunted by long hours of pain
Did they struggle against the wild waters in vain?

While *we* slumbered all free from the pitiless cold,
Was it then that death came to those mariners bold?
When the gloom was around them of storm and of night
Did they moor their life-barks in Eternity's light?

We knew not, nor will know, how perished those men,
The best of our islands, who came not again,
We but know that they trusted their lives to the wave,
And the treacherous ocean, false friend, was their grave.

AFTER THE STORM.

THE fitful storm had passed away,
　　Its driving wind and rain
Had swept o'er earth for many a day,
　　And left her fair again.

I stood upon a low hillside
　　And viewed the tranquil scene.
The island rose in verdant pride,
From out the ever-changing tide,
　　Like some mermaiden queen.

The glistening dew hung on the grass
　　Like tears from angels' eyes ;
And ocean, like a sea of glass,
　　Smiled back to the calm skies.
No trace was left of that wild storm,
　　Save where some ruin lies,
For nature's worn and wearied form
　　Reposed in mildest guise.

I see it yet, that beauteous scene—
    The gently sloping hill,
The young lambs frisking on the green,
    The peewits screaming shrill,
The rocks of hoar majestic mien,
    The ocean deep and still ;—

The churchyard in the little vale,
    The moaning murmuring waves,
Whose melancholy echoes wail
    Beside those lonely graves.

And one sleeps there whose lamp of life
    Went out ere it was noon ;
She feared to meet the coming strife,
    The battle fraught with terrors rife.
So yielded up her maiden life,
    So softly and so soon.

And side by side beneath a knowe
    Four brothers young are sleeping.
They withered from the parent bough
    Like fruit that's ripe for reaping.

I lingered by the churchyard wall
Looking upon those mounds so small—

So small, and yet that held so much'
That once had felt life's kindling touch ;
And I thought that they, in those cold graves,
Seemed like the weeds tossed by the waves
    Upon the peaceful shore,
Never to rise with the restless motion
That heaves the pulse of the mighty ocean,
    Never, oh ! never more.
While we, like the weeds that still ebb and flow
With the sea as it paces to and fro,
    We mingle in the strife ;
But they sleep on in their island graves,
Their requiem sung by the passing waves,
    All heedlessly of life.

From them the storm had passed away,
    Its driving wind and rain,
But I knew a time would come when they
    Would be all fair again.

The rosy hue of evening's sky
    Seemed like a promise true,
That they would rise one day to fly
    Beyond its boundless blue.

MAGGIE.

SHE grew up like a silent flower,
　Beside our northern water,
Sheltered by love from every care,
　Her father's only daughter.

Before her girlish presence bent,
　The heart of each young brother;
She gladdened home with tenderness,
　This first-born of her mother.

A keen wind came with biting frost,
　It touched this fav'rite blossom.
It paled her cheek and chilled her blood.
　And cankered in her bosom.

She bent before that biting blast,
　Which to her heart's core quivered;
She loved her island home—yet past
　As rose by storm winds shivered.

They bore her hence in hope and fear,
   Across the northern water;
They dreamed that summer climes would save
   Their cherished only daughter.

Yet drooped she still; and one dark day
   Her spirit pure departed,
And left a home bereft of light,
   And parents broken hearted.

Back to her native isle they bore
   The soul's sweet casket rifled;
And all the love that once was hers,
   Down in their hearts they stifled.

They meekly laid their flower to rest
   Beside the northern water,
And bowed their heads, and drooped their hands,
   For *God* had ta'en their daughter.

HEL-YA-WATER.

WHERE the sod is bleak and barren.
  And the haunted hillocks lie ;
Where the gloomy Hel-ya-water
  Looks up blackly to the sky ;
Where the mists are ever brooding.
  And the plover's whistle shrill,
Is the only sound that echoes
  O'er the sombre silent hill.

Where the waves of Hel-ya-water
  Break around one little Isle,
That in fresh and verdant beauty
  Ventured often-times to smile,
There the raven built its eyrie,
  There it reared its savage brood ;
And the young lambs from the common.
  Were the nestlings' dainty food.

Year by year that hoary raven
　　Made the haunted spot his rest :
Year by year upon the island
　　Brooded he upon his nest ;
And no man would ever venture
　　To invade the lone domain,
Where in solitary grandeur
　　The proud bird was wont to reign.

It was Yule time, and the cottars ,
　　Lit the joyous Christmas fires,
And they filled the wassail goblet,
　　As in old times did their sires.
There was mirth in every dwelling,
　　And the song and jest went round,
And the laugh, the dance, the music,
　　Rose above the tempest's sound.

Oh ! the winds are raging wildly,
　　And the clouds are drifting by ;
'Tis the night when Trows are revelling
　　By the Hel-ya-water nigh.
Then who is he will venture,
　　Where the visitants unseen
Trace their weird and magic circles
　　On the blooming island's green ?

There the dismal bird of evil
   Is rejoicing with the storm ;
Who will dare to-night, and conquer,
   The old raven's sable form ?
Who will dare to go and vanquish
   The fierce bird of night and gloom !
Who will dare the spells of magic ?
   Who will bear to him his doom ?

See, young Yaspar's eye is blazing
   With the fires, so fleet and free ;
Son of many an ancient sea-king,
   Son of Norse men bold was he.
Forth against the stormy tempest,
   Forth against the blinding snow,
Forth in all his youthful manhood,
   Went the raven's boyish foe.

Cold the surf of Hel-ya-water
   Frets around the raven's nest ;
But the boy is rising bravely
   On each puny wavelet's crest.
See, how boldly now he ventures,
   He has won the haunted isle,
Where, in calm and lofty silence,
   Waits the lonely bird the while.

Thick and fast now fall the snowflakes,
　Shrouding valley, *voe*,* and hill ;
Yelling round the Hel-ya-water
　Flit the spirits of all ill.
Hark, the solitary plover
　Wails a note of death and woe,
And a cry of anguish answers
　From the watery depths below.

———

Morning breaks,—a snow-shroud covers
　All the drear deserted earth ;
In young Yaspar's home is weeping,
　There are mourners by his hearth.
By the haunted Hel-ya-water,
　Sleeps the bold boy in his grave,
And the islet's ancient inmate,
　Is entombed beneath the wave.

" Voe "—A fiord or arm of the sea running far inland.

THE SEA-GULL'S SONG

TO THE RETURNING FISHERMAN.

FOLLOW me, follow me, whither I lead thee,
  Nor let the mermaidens thy fancy allure,
For further and further away I must speed me,
  Oh! haste then, and follow a guide that is sure.

The day is fast fading, the night's coming on,
  Dim shines my home-star in the distance away;
I've wandered and wandered, but now must be gone,
  My gentle mate pineth that still I delay.

Far, where the rocks darkly frown over the sea,
  Where Hialtland's dear isles in their beauty repose,
There, friend, is the loved home where speedily we
  Shall rest from the toils which with evening will close.

'Tis days since I led thee across the deep wave,
  Together we've sailed o'er the ocean so blue,
I saw that a sigh to the breezes ye gave,
  As the hills of our country were lost to our view.

But soon yon dear isle will again greet our sight,
　So give to the sea-sprites each sorrowing sigh,
The beacons, by love lit, shine clearly and bright.
　Then give to the ocean that tear in thine eye.

Haste ! wider and wider spread out to the wind
　Yon sail that is fluttering as if to be free,
And soon we will leave laggard billows behind—
　The waves cannot bound half so quickly as we.

See how gladly the helm obeyeth thy will,
　And see how thy bark from her prow flings the spray :
She dasheth along like a wild wayward rill
　That hasteth through all to the ocean away.

　　　　*　　　*　　　*　　　*

My pinions are weary ; our journey was long,
　But the sight of yon isle cheers my spirit again,
Then loud let thy voice join the heart-thrilling song
　That welcomes us back from the troublous main.

　　　　*　　　*　　　*　　.　*

Now furl thy sail, let thy hand cease its toil,
　Thy bark has at length reached the long-looked-for
　　shore,
Thy foot has again touched the dear island soil,
　And wistful eyes welcome thee back evermore.

And now to my nest that looks down on the sea,
   And my mate that broods fondly, away I must fly :
So fare-thee-well, friend, love-lit eyes watch for me;
   Oh ! where is the bird that's as happy as I.

HOME AT LAST.

I.

I SANG a song of the bounteous sea,
  I sang to my babe asleep,
I sang of the lad that was dear to me,
  Whose boat was out on the deep.
I sang of the boat with her shining sail,
  Of the crew that were staunch and brave,
Of the ocean gifts that would grace their "hale"—
  I sang this song of the wave.

I sang my song to his slumbering child,
  And the surf which crept to the door,
Replied to my voice with a murmur mild,
  And then to our threshold bore
The bonnie boat with her blithesome crew,
  With the lad that was dear to me,
And the babe it opened its eyes of blue,
  And I sang no more of the sea.

II.

I looked abroad on the sullen sea,
   I looked far out one day,
And "What keeps the boat with my lad from me?"
   I asked of the fretful spray.
The surges swept o'er the weeded strand,
   And the message they seemed to bring,
Was "Pluck away from a widowed hand
   The wife's fair marriage-ring."

I knelt in prayer, for a boding fear
   Had come to my laden heart,
And I found how I held him *more* than dear,
   And how hard it would be to part.
At last one came with a saddened face,
   And said that the angry sea
Had 'whelmed the boat in her matchless race—
   And the lad that was dear to me.

III.

I wailed aloud by the treacherous sea,
   And they bade me cease my moan,
And turn to the babe that was left with me,
   And know I was not alone.
Ah! how could I bid my eyes not weep,
   Or stifle my mad despair,
When I knew that the restless roving deep
   Was lifting *his* chestnut hair?

.

How could I raise my stricken head,
  Or hearken to comfort's tone,
When I knew that his shifting couch was made
  Where the spirits of ocean moan—
When I knew that his form was tossed about
  At the will of the wanton wave ;
When I knew that the savage surges' shout
  Was the dirge of my bonnie brave ?

IV.

I listened alone to the sound of the sea,
  And I shivered with sickening woe,
For I thought that the voice that was dear to me
  Had spoke in the water's flow.
I felt that his soul could find no rest
  While drifting, unburied, lay
The dear dead form that so late had blest
  My home with love's lightsome ray.

I cowered and trembled with anguish dread,
  For the wind, as it winnowed by,
Took the wishful tone of the drownéd dead,
  And echoed his spirit's sigh.
I could not silence my sorrow's sound,
  And I called to the ravening sea,
" Give back what is mine, that in hallowed ground
  I may lay what was dear to me."

V.

They wandered at eve by the fickle sea,
   And down by the weeded strand,
Whose brown fringe circles the sunny lea,
   And his barklet was wont to land.
On that rugged beach, by the cottage door.
   And (ah! do I live to tell?)
They found him laid on the fretted shore.
   By the home he had loved so well.

The guardian angel that watched his birth
   Had guided the helpless clay
To a resting-place on its native earth,
   And silent and calm he lay.
Wet, wet and pale, was the poor wan brow
   That came from the faithless sea,
But I cried, "Thank God there is pure peace now
   For the soul that was dear to me."

My Dear Papa—It was at your suggestion that the above verses were written. You made me acquainted with our weird old fancy of the souls of the drowned finding no rest until the poor remnant of mortality had been buried or dissolved into the elements. You drew a vivid picture of the scene where the lost fisherman's body was found. Too true it is that the poor fellow was tossed up at his widow's home. Too true are all the incidents above recorded; but it was your whispered talk by the fire one night that bade me record the sad tale in verse, and therefore to you I dedicate the poem.

HALLOWE'EN.

ON Hallowmas-e'en, when the moon's pale light.
Is streaming down on the haunted height;
When the magic circles of fadeless green
Are glisteningly gemmed by the dew-drop's sheen :
When the waves are as calm as a sea of glass,
And the sky is still, save for clouds that pass
Their shadows stealthily over the grass.

When the earth and ocean have gone to rest,
When babes are asleep on the mother-breast,
When lovers are dreaming of days to come,
When the sailor thinks of his distant home,
When flowers have folded their little leaves,
When birds are nestled 'neath heather eaves,
And her mystical spells the midnight weaves.

When nothing that's born of the sea or land,
Is waking to tell of the elfin band,
Who merrily dance by the " fairy ring,"
Who gambol about and gleefully sing,

And flit and caper as long as they may;
For 'tis but short time till the coming day
Shall hasten them all from the hill away.

Those light little fairies, all draped in green,
May trip o'er the hillocks on Hallowmas-e'en,
Their innocent pranks they are free to play,
But woe to the mortal who comes that way;
Dominion they have o'er that midnight hour,
For Hallowmas-rites are their earthly dower,
And the changeling art is within their power.

Alas for the maid who goes out that night,
There's a witchy gleam in the flickering light;
Woe, woe, to the mother who leaves alone
Her rosy-cheeked babe by her threshold stone:
And woe to the sage who shall fail to bring
The charms that protect, to the fairy ring,
Where those tiny spirits so merrily sing.

On Hallowmas-even, all good folk say,
The fairies have pow'r o'er each bright night-ray;
They may flit around while the moonbeams shine,
And pass at will o'er the mystic line,
Which circles their home on the heathery hill,
And binds them from wandering on deeds of ill
On *other eves* when the world is still.

So when Hallowmas-e'en comes round once more,
Forbid all to venture outside your door,
Weave secret charms, and no sprite will come
To play his pranks by your cottage home ;
And oh ! be sure that you never dare
To go to the hill when the fairies wear
Their emerald mantles as light as air,
And dance away every elfin care.

THE LAST OF HIS NAME.

A THUNDER-CLOUD hung over head.
  And large dull raindrops fell—
'Twas nature's tribute to the dead,
  Her wild funereal knell.

Beneath an arch of hoary trees
  There paused a mourning band ;
They brought from out his ancient home,
  The master of the land.

They lingered, as if loth to bear
  The honoured form away,
Not one of all his name was left,
  Save that poor lifeless clay.

Without, the walls of the old house
  By bending boughs were swept ;
Within, in silence and alone
  A childless widow wept.

E

With solemn steps the mourners hied
  Towards the rugged shore,
Where on the leaden billows ride
A fleet of barklets tempest-tried,
  With muffled oar on oar.

From sorrowing sea-girt sister isles,
  His peers have gathering come,
And humbler friends are also there.
Swelling the train of them that bear
  The laird to his last home.

The skiff *his* hand had loved to guide,
  O'er ocean's wrinkled face,
Was launched once more for him, and *there*
  With reverend care they place
The burden they had borne so far,—
  The last of the old race.

The frowning crags spread forth their arms
  Of sombre, sea-worn gray,
As up the voe the shallops glide,
  And cleave their wavy way.

No sound was there to break the calm,
  Save the weird wailing cry

Of wild birds, and the restless roar
    Of surf in caverns nigh.

And sad and slow the silent train
    Floats o'er the wearied waves.
Whose briny bosoms rise and fall
Beside the churchyard's ruined wall.
    Where are his fathers' graves.

They laid him down in that lone spot.
    A dreary time-worn place,
And left him where his kindred lie—
    The last of the old race.

THE SEA-GIRT HOME.

WHERE do the stormy seas
  Sparkle in foam?
Where fiercely blows the breeze
  From Northland come?
Where lowers the cloudy sky?
Where mounts the eagle high?
  By my loved home.

Where do the Vikings sleep
  In the wild bay?
Where do the mermaids keep
  Their watch all day?
Where doth Aurora shine?
O'er that dear home of mine
  Far, far, away.

Where do the heather hills
  Rise brown and bare?
Where flow the tiny rills
  Freshly and fair?

Where do the heath-flowers blow
Under the pure cold snow?
 My home—'tis there.

Where do the sea-birds light
 On swift wings flee?
Where do the rocks like night
 Frown on the sea?
Where doth each high-arched cave
Entomb some warrior brave,
 Once strong and free?

Where do the sun's dim smiles
 Glint o'er the lea?
'Tis where lone Thule's isles
 Rest on the sea;
'Tis where the billows roar
Around my native shore,
 Where I would be.

Sport on, ye foamy waves,
 Wildly sublime;
Still frown, ye rocks and caves,
 Braving old time;
Blow, breezes, fresh and free:
Guard well, O glorious sea.
 My native clime.

BIRDS OF OMEN.

ON his mighty wing of ebon
    Comes the bird of night,
Not upon the misty hilltop
    Does he stay his flight.
Spurning valley, rock, and ocean,
    All before him spread,
Slowly on his dusky pinion,
    Laves he overhead.

Where the fisher's home is freshened
    By the passing wave,
Hoarsely bodes the warning raven
    Of a watery grave.
Quickly from the lowly dwelling
    Comes the cottar's wife,
Looks she out where ocean beareth
    All she loves in life.

Not a ripple stirs the bosom
    Of the tranquil sea ;

Not a breath of wind comes sighing
    From the verdant lea.
Hark ! she hears the dismal croaking,
    And her cheek grows pale,
Wistful glances sends she seaward
    Searching for *his* sail.

Now the spectre bird of omen,
    Dark as midnight's gloom,
Hovers, uttering weirdlike warning
    Of a coming doom.
And the startled wife in terror
    Clasps her little child,
And beholds a tempest gathering
    Where so late all smiled.

Downward roll the awful thunders,
    Answering ocean's roar ;
Madly rave the angry breezes
    Round the rocky shore ;
Wildly scream the frighted sea-birds
    By their island cave ;
Swiftly close the wakened waters
    O'er the fisher's grave.

Solemnly departs the raven
    On his sable wing.

Joying that his baleful presence
    Could such sorrow bring.
Blackness reigns within that cottage,
    And the weepers dwell
Where the croaker shrieked of evil,
    Where his shadow fell.

   *   *   *   *

On a snowy wing of silence,
    From the distant hill,
Gleaming pure as white-robed spirit.
    In the evening still,
Comes the lonely owlet, bearing
    Death to broken hearts,
And he haunts the house whence sorrow
    Never more departs.

Round the cot on stealthy pinion
    Flits Minerva's bird,
And the dying wife rejoices,
    And her soul is stirred,
When she hears the hooting nigh her.
    Of that being weird,
And she answers to his calling
    With a kindly word.

" Welcome," says she, " well I know thee,
    Phantom bird of snow,

From thy solitary dwelling
  Come to tell me, go ;
Thou hast come to give my spirit
  From its woes release,
Thou hast come to bid mine anguished
  Bosom be at peace ;
Welcome, welcome ; *now* the aching
  At my heart will cease."

Silently, as shadow falling
  From a wand'ring cloud,
Went the owlet back to Norland,
  Wrapped in downy shroud ;
And upon the arctic mountain
  Where the bleak winds moan,
Full of melancholy dreamings,
  Broods he all alone.

Troubled breakers dash tumultuous
  O'er the fisher's breast ;
On the grave, where sleeps the widow,
  Pale flowers meekly rest ;
Gloomy silence fills the homestead
  By the sounding surge ;
On the cliff the boding raven
  Croaks a dismal dirge.

THE CHANGELING.

WHY lingers the child by the cold hearth-stone.
When her sisters twain to the shore have gone
To watch for their father's returning sail?
Oh! why are her features so wan and pale?

Why does her eye ever hold a tear?
Why trembles her lip with a look of fear?
Why, heedless of mother and father's ire,
Still broods she alone by the waning fire?

She had wandered out on a sunny day,
To watch on the hill-side the lambs at play;
She had strayed o'er the heathery hillock's side.
And the grass-strewn valley so smooth and wide.

A mist had come from the dreary swamp,
And folded the child in its mantle damp;
Had shrouded the hill and the valley fair,
And with diamond-dews decked her sunny hair.

She had wandered on till her weary feet
Had paused, spell-bound by the magic seat,
Where the fairy queen and her elfin train
Were weaving rare pearls of the mist and rain.

What the fair child saw on that lonely height,
Was never meant to meet mortal sight ;
And the wrathful sprites, in their anger wild,
Wreaked vengeance dark on the simple child.

When the morning came, and the light of day,
Chased the misty clouds from the hill away,
The friends who had weepingly sought for found
The damsel asleep on enchanted ground.

They carried her home to their humble cot,
But the direful spells of the magic spot,
Still hung o'er her weak and bewildered brain,
And cast on her features a look of pain.

Her sisters try to awake her glee,
Her brothers gaze on her pityingly,
Her father prays she may soon find rest,
Her mother fondles her to her breast.

But day and night, by the cold hearth-stone
She sits and dreams by herself alone,

No word she utters, no sweet smile wears,
She seems so burdened with hidden cares.

Her bosom will garner its load of woe,
Her tears will come in a ceaseless flow,
Her tongue will be mute, and that look of pain
Will live on her face, till the fairy train
Lift off from her spirit their spell-wrought chain.

THE CAPTIVE SEA-BIRD.

CHILD of the ocean ! what dims thine eye,
Whose light once shone like a summer sky !
Does thy head bend down from the flaunting rays
Of the glorious sun that around thee plays?
Oh no ! thy heart joys in those sunny beams,
For thy bowed head rises to greet their gleams.

Beautiful bird, I have tended thee well,
I have made thee a home in a shady dell,
In a garden fair, with the flowers and trees,
To shield thee, my bird, from each angry breeze.
Not a breath can ruffle one glossy plume,
Then why is thine aspect so filled with gloom ?

I took thee away from thy parent nest.
Ere thy heart had tasted the wind's unrest,
Ere thy wings had learned to bear thee along
In freedom and joy like an angel's song ;
And I brought thee here ere thy parent sea
Had taught thee how sweet it is to be free.

It grieves me to gaze on thy fading eye,
To see thee in sorrow and sadness die.
I have loved thee well, and with tender care
I've treasured and prized thee, my bright and fair ;
Oh ! tell me the cause of thy heart's deep woe.
Child of the ocean, why is it so ?

" Restore me again to my rocky home,
Lashed by the wild waves, kissed by the foam.
Let me look on the storm raging around,
Let me list to the waves as they proudly bound.
Let me soar on pinions unfettered, free,
And mine eye will brighten with hope and glee.

"Oh ! what though your sunniest flowers bloom nigh,
And what though the sun gilds the laughing sky ?
I can see my brethren on aerial wing,
Float light on the breath of the genial spring.
Or coyly skim o'er the world of sea,
"Tis with them, with them, that I fain would be.

" Oh ! long, long ago in a distant cave,
I was lulled to sleep by a murmuring wave.
It whispered of freedom I know not here,
Of freedom and joy that can feel no fear,
It taught me a love for that wild rude home,
Can ye wonder then that I long to roam.

" Restore me again to that home of mine,
And my heart no longer in grief will pine ;
Let me fly to my rocks by the rolling sea,
On tameless wing and with spirit free.
Oh ! open my prison and let me go,
And my eye will gleam and my glad song flow."

MY MOTHER'S ROOM.

WHENEVER I think of my childhood,
And the home where my young days sped.
I remember one room of all others
With its quaintly old curtained bed.

The invalid chair by the fire-place,
And the phials that told a sad tale
Of much patient and weary suffering,
Of a bright face wasted and pale.

So far as my thoughts go backward,
I remember that same old room,
Now filled with young hearts and their gladness.
Now shrouded in sickness and gloom.

It was *there* where we all were cradled,
It was *there* little sister died,
It was *there* that our mother wept for
One lost in his young life's pride.

It was there in the Sabbath evenings
 That we clustered around her chair,
To listen to lessons of kindness,
 And to Bible-stories and prayer.

It was there that we carried our burdens,
 And poured into sympathy's ear ;
The grief that comes often to childhood
 Comes laden with hope as with fear.

It was there, where, in silent sorrow,
 We helplessly gathered around,
And mutely, with aching hearts, listened
 To pain's agonised, stifled sound.

It was there, when in life's glad morning,
 That I came to my mother's side,
And she knew that her child no longer
 Was hers, for one claimed her his bride.

It was there, in the early winter,
 That the flower of our spring oped its eyes,
Like a primrose of fairest beauty,
 Or a violet of rarest dyes ;

And my mother carried the blossom,
 And laid in my arms to rest

F

My living, my beautiful floweret,
   The first-born bird of my nest.

And there, in that same old chamber,
   I learn'd, what each woman must know,
That no fountain of love runs deeper,
   Or so fondly, freely, doth flow,
As a mother's love for her children,
   Through happiness, peril, and woe.

So thus, when I think of my childhood,
   And the home where my young days sped,
I remember above all others
   One room and its quaint old bed.

THE THREE PETS.

A FUNNY, frisky terrier, in tawny-coloured coat.
And restless eye of hazel hue that doth each move-
ment note ;
In very truth *one* hazel eye, and bright as autumn
star,
The other lost he long ago in some disastrous war.

A Persian pussy, sleek as silk, who sits beside my
chair, .
And, purring peacefully, smooths down some rudely-
rumpled hair,
Or perched upon my shoulder, with a look so soft
and sly,
Regards my slice of buttered toast with half-shut
envious eye.

A tiny toddling trotty, who comes prattling to my side,
To tell of broken dolls, or on my knee to have a ride :

Who waits but to receive and give sweet childhood's
  loving kiss,
Who pulls my heart-strings out of tune ten times a-
  day, I wiss.

When morning brings my porridge-plate they hasten
  to my side,
And *five* keen eyes are watching then my breakfast to
  divide.
Miss Puss would claim the cup of cream, and doggie
  wants the dish,
While Lalla clamours for the whole, and—well, *she* gets
  her wish.

A rough-clad roystering terrier; an eastern beauty,
  drest
In mottled robe of silken fur, and ermine-mantled
  breast;
The doggie curls up at my foot, and pussy on mine
  arm,
But Lalla nestles near my heart, *her* love its chiefest
  charm.

THE ANGEL VISITANT.

"WHITHER did you wander, sister?
    Why were you so long away?
I have sought you, far and often,
    Wondering why you'd still delay;
Sister, tell me, gentle sister,
    Where you lingered all the day.

" Nigh the tender star of morning,
    Nigh the strong proud king of night,
Hovering o'er the belt of Saturn,
    Or by Mars the calm and bright,
On Orion's glittering girdle,
    I had sought thy form of light.

" I had tuned each golden harp-chord
    To a melody divine,
And the flowers that live for ever
    I had wreathed in garlands fine,
Thinking that such wiles would bring thee
    Back to this fond heart of mine.

Did you wander, spirit-sister,
    Where bright stars more distant shine ?"

" Brother ! thou knowest well I love thee
    As the bridegroom loves the bride,
But I love yet more the Saviour
    Who for our redemption died ;
And I would remind thee, dearest,
    We have other loves beside.

" Ere we came to this calm haven,
    Where the faint of spirit rest,
I was wont to still my sorrows
    On a mother's loving breast ;
And a father's tender blessing
    Was the boon I loved the best.

" In that world, whose milder radiance
    We can scarcely now descry
'Mong the myriad hosts that hasten
    Through the still, blue, boundless sky,
Lived we once with sisters, brothers,
    One fond band of unity.

" You remember that dear homestead,
    Where we lived in joy and peace,

Ere the time came, when those love-links,
  With which all were bound, did cease—
Cease to hold us in *one* dwelling;
  You and I soon found release.

" But I often would be thinking
  Of the eyes that watched my youth,
Still would treasure the sweet lessons
  Taught to me of heavenly truth,
By that wisest, fondest mother,
Who still mourns for us, my brother.

" And my heart would long to see her,
  And I fain would downwards fly,
To behold those friends of childhood
  In that home beyond the sky.
I have seen them, and they knew not
  That their long-lost loved was nigh.

" I have hovered round their footsteps,
  I have fanned my father's face,
I have held my darling mother
  In a spirit's wan embrace.

" I have seen a tender infant
  Lying where I once did lie,

And that cherub, late from heaven,
   Only saw the angel nigh.
No one knew why smiled the baby,
   Or what fixed his wand'ring eye.

" And our parents, bending softly
   O'er this new-found darling's nest,
Wondered why so oft and eager
   Turned he from each tender breast,
Ever looking upward, upward,
   Always smiling *there* the best.

" No one knew a child of Heaven
   Watched above the little bed,
No one saw the sainted infant
   Hovering o'er the little head,
No one deemed the spirit nigh them,
   Of one long to earth-love dead.

" Thus I lingered near the baby,
   And when baby-like he wept,
As a breath of summer music
   O'er his fluttering heart I swept ;
Calmed his every fear and fancy,
   Soothed him till he smiled and slept.
This, my brother, was the mission
   That so long me from thee kept."

" Oh ! how blest thou wast, my sister ;
 But must I still look and wait ?
Will those dear ones soon be coming ?
 Shall we meet them at the gate ?
Will the babe come with the rest ?"
" Brother ! God doth all things best."

ANGEL CHORUS.

Guard and guide, O gracious Father !
 On the earth thy little flock,
Blessed Saviour, be thou ever
 Their salvation's firm-built rock,
May they tread the path to Heaven,
And all praise to Thee be given !

You will not have forgotten, dear mamma, how, when my little Harry was a baby, he was wont to gaze up at one particular part of that dear old roof which covers *the* room of many memories. You remember how I could always still his crying by turning him to look in that direction, and how we all did wonder at the strange baby-fancy. I have tried to explain it in my own fashion, for I think that you also love to think of the parted as "ever hovering near." Let me dedicate the imperfect poem to the "mother of angels" and my own kind mamma.

I BLESS the sweet sun-picture that has come
    across the main,
Giving thoughts that dwell in memory a golden-gilded
    rein.
I bless the kindly countenance that can our heart's
    love draw,
Who is everybody's auntie, if she's nobody's mamma.

Her smile is brightly winning yet, and oh ! her silver
    hair
Was bleached by thought for others' good, and other
    people's care.
A soul of true unselfish love has made her life's
    unrest,
For everybody's auntie has a mother's anxious breast.

The little children come to her to show their tiny
    toys,
Youth tells her sympathising ear its love—both hopes
    and joys ;

The heart of man, o'erwrought by toil, has laid his
    burden down
By everybody's auntie, and *there* found the Christian's
    crown.

Lone woman's grief her voice hath soothed ; the weary
    working one
Hath left her side with buoyant step the race to
    bravely run.
Her hand has led the wavering feet, and smoothed
    the dismal way
That leads from life's tumultuous strife to God's
    eternal day.

Across the wave for weary miles is stretched her
    gentle wand ;
Her chain of love has flowery links in many a distant
    land :
It girds the strong, the weak, the old, the young, the
    good and brave,
And twines its tender cords of love as fondly round
    the grave.

Her brooding breast has shelter given to many a
    lonesome bird,
Whose fluttering heart, and half-fledged wing, her
    spirit's pity stirred.

'Twas love, all love, that bade her thus obey fond
 nature's law;
And everybody's auntie has been all the world's
 mamma.

Young hands are waking heavenly harps among the
 seraph throng;
It was her voice that taught them here to learn the
 angel's song.
Earth's saints there are in heaven, who breathe her
 name in every prayer,
Who 'guard her mortal way, who long to bid her
 welcome there.

God bless our gentle auntie, now her evening hour is
 near,
And may the setting sun still gild her pathway calm
 and clear!
While life, and woe, and earth, go on, we need the
 winning hand
Of everybody's auntie, to lead to the Fatherland.

THE PICTURE ON THE WALL.

THEY haunt me aye those dreamy eyes—
They bear a message from the skies ;
And I have gazed upon them, till
My heart's desire rose o'er my will,
And I have wished, with all its pain,
That he were back to earth again.
Oh ! I have looked upon that brow,
Whose light is all immortal now,
Till pride and love have told my heart
How high had been his glorious part,
Had death not plucked his spirit-form
   For ever from life's strife and storm.

It haunts my soul, that young bright face,
And yet my memory cannot trace
One lineament she holdeth dear,
One fond remembrance treasured here.
Sometimes across my thought there strays
A shadowy form, with earnest gaze,
Whose eyes are like those eyes that gleam
Upon me with that lustrous beam ;

Whose broad white brow of treasured thought
Resembles this, so weirdly wrought
Upon my heart by night and day,
And never turns its light away.

When fireside shadows flickering fall
Upon the Picture on the Wall,
They seem to flit about in strife,
As if they sought to give it life;
And when I look, the dreamy eyes
Seem lit with soul-beams from within,
And laughter-wreaths, in glorious guise,
Dance round the lips whose words could win
Where'er they went.   Ah me! ah me!
For fancy's strange wild witchery.

One Christmas-eve we decked the room
With green leaves born by winter's gloom,
And when I placed the ivy bough
Above that brightly beauteous brow,
Methought a smile returned the gaze
I cast upon the pictured face;
And then I thought, as low I leant,
His soul a whispered message sent,
And for one moment, heart and mind
Seemed in communion with the dead;

And thoughts, before so dark and blind,
For ever from my spirit fled ;
And I could to my bosom tell
'Twas heaven's own hand that on him fell,
And Jesus doeth all things well.

I have no memory of the time
When, called to yonder treacherous clime,
He sailed across the dismal main,
And never smiled on us again.
He left upon mine infant brow   .
A tender kiss, whose impress now
I pray had stamped some feature rare
Of his, that I might find it there ;
I would that *thus* they could recall
The face that's pictured on the wall.
Time flutters past.   Each scene, each face,
Changes with time's unheeding race ;
But still, from out its gilded frame,
That face looks calmly forth—the same.
I ventured forth the fight to share,
And, hasting back, I found *it* there,
In the same place serenely fair—
Still looking at me, smiling still
Through every change of good and ill.

O how it haunts me !   In the night
I see those eyes of living light ;
I hear a voice whose touching tone
Ne'er fell in life upon mine ear ;
And when I sit me down alone,
I seem to feel his presence near.
I think, if guardian spirits come
To guide us hence, he leads me home :
I think, if angels are allowed
To visit this terrestial ball,
That his bright wings have often bowed
Beside his Picture on the Wall.

BABY LALLA.

'TWAS a day in spring when our darling came.
  She came with the first fair flowers:
A blossom of promise, a flow'ret rare,
  A sunbeam to gild dark hours.

She seemeth to me like the fragrant breeze
  That follows on April showers :
And holy and pure as the angels be,
  Is this dear daughter of ours.

She nestles herself in our inmost hearts—
  Our bird in its own home bower—
And there she will reign like a queen for aye.
  Her love our heart's richest dower.

Oh ! treasures of earth may elude our path,
  And life's darkest clouds may lower,
But, having jewels that are heavenly gifts,
  From naught will we shrink or cower ;

But with grateful joy bless the Father hand
  That gives to our love such flowers,
As He who first woke in us parent love.
  And this dear daughter of ours.

GRANDPAPA'S PET.

A WEE romping toddling thing,
Peeping from the mother-wing,
Scarcely more than baby yet,
Grandpapa's own little pet.

Smiling lip, and merry eye,
Voice of choicest melody,
Heart aglow with love's own fire,
Pattering feet that never tire.

Little hands, so small and fat,
Rosy cheeks we love to pat,
Sunny spirit, sunny hair,
Shedding sunshine everywhere.

Sturdy form of childish grace,
Flitting aye from place to place ;
Ne'er at rest till evening brings
Gentle sleep on golden wings.

Prattling tongue that ripples on.
Like some echo sweetly lone ;
Asking questions that surprise,
Uttering wisdom strangely wise.

Following wheresoe'er we rove,
With a child's confiding love,
Weeping, smiling soon again,
Sunshine gleaning up the rain.

Laying down his little head,
When his simple prayer is said,
When the hour has come for rest,
Dreaming dreams by angels blest.

But before he goes to sleep,   .
To his slumber soft and deep,
Grandpapa comes in to get
Kisses from his little pet.

THE ECHO IN THE HOUSE.

THERE'S a flutter of leaves above me,
    And a bending of boughs around,
And under my feet the green grass
    Is making a rustling sound.

There's a twitter of drowsy sparrows,
    And a lark's late vesper hymn,
And a sunbeam saying " good-even "
    To the foliage dense and dim.

There's the gable of the old homestead
    Peering from out the trees,
And I sit, and enraptured hearken
    To the sounds borne by the breeze.

For the old house bears in its bosom
    An echo subdued and sweet,
Like the sigh that a world-weary spirit
    Will heave for life's pleasures fleet.

It comes to me now, that echo,
  And it ripples the silent air,
As a pebble we throw at random
  Will ruffle the brooklet fair.

It bears on its gentle harp-strings
  The tone of a child's young voice,
And the patter of eager footsteps,
  And laughter, and warblings choice.

But a time has been when that echo
  Bore forth from the old home's heart
A wail of disease and sorrow,
  A plaint from the wounds that smart.

A time *has been*, but oh ! never,
  I pray that the echo old
May breathe in its tender cadence
  Such tales as too oft it told.

"LADY ELLA."

LADY Ella, lithe and lightsome,
   With a wealth of nut-brown hair,
And a forehead smooth and lofty,
   Like a bit of marble rare;
Lady Ella, Lady Ella,
      Bright and fair.

Lady Ella, good and gentle,
   With an eye of beaming blue,
And a cheek so soft and dimpled,
   And a lip of ruddy hue;
Lady Ella, Lady Ella,
      Kind and true.

Lady Ella, always singing
   Like a lark in sunny June;
Always dreaming, always beaming
   Like a tender harvest-moon;
Lady Ella, Lady Ella,
      In life's noon.

Lady Ella, sweet and smiling,
   Skilled in all a woman's arts,
Brightening with her little presence
   Even earth's most darkened parts :
Lady Ella, Lady Ella,
        Queen of hearts.

Lady Ella, most unselfish,
   Thinking all of others' woes,
Never sparing foot or finger
   In the cause of friends or foes ;
Lady Ella, Lady Ella,
        Thornless rose.

Lady Ella, surely blessings
   Circle halo-like your head,
Surely flowers of heavenly sending
   Bloom beneath your airy tread ;
Lady Ella, Lady Ella,
        Angel-led.

FIRESIDE FANCIES.

I.

SITTING by the fire,
      With the winter winds without,
      And a glad child's merry shout
      Ringing through the silent house,
      Like the tender tuneful voice
                  Of a lyre.

II.

Sitting by the fire,
      With no light but that which falls
      On the dusky chamber-walls
      From the changing fitful beams
      That throw out their lurid gleams,
                  As in ire.

III.

Sitting by the fire.
      With hands crossed on idle knee,
      Gazing, gazing dreamily,

On the flickering flames that glow.
Brightly, wildly, swift and slow,
> Then expire.

IV.

Sitting by the fire,
Viewing in each ember bright,
And in every red flame's light,
Faces, figures, strange and quaint ;
Some I know, some far and faint,
> And some nigher.

V.

Sitting by the fire,
Seeing wondrous landscapes there—
Lofty mountains, meadows fair,
Burning islands, gorgeous skies,
Salamandrin forms that rise
> High and higher.

VI.

Sitting by the fire,
Watching how the sparks ascend,
How they glimmer, how they end,
As the dreams of early youth,
Of whose smouldering ashes truth
> Raised a pyre.

VII.

Sitting by the fire,
> Piling firebrands one by one,
> Till their ruddy life is done ;
> As we reared in days of yore
> Hopes and visions, lovelit lore,
>> Fond desire.

VIII.

Sitting by the fire,
> Looking at the steadfast glow
> Of the brands that burn below,
> Like the pure and earnest flame
> That with riper seasons came,
>> Bringing nigher
> · Love and hope, and heavenly dreams,
> Summer sunshine, golden beams.
> Ah ! the fire falls faint and low.
> *Thus* our lifetimes flit and flow,
>> And expire.
> Thus we dream, and thus we die,
> Thus at last we bid good-bye
>> To life's fire.

BED-TIME.

BABY-FACES, clean and bright,
Little figures robed in white,
Voices lisping forth "good-night."

Golden-tinted well-brushed hair,
Shading foreheads smooth and fair,
Folded fingers, infant prayer.

Eyelids drooped o'er sleepy eyes,
As the midnight hides the skies,
Veiling all their azure dyes.

Bright young heads laid down to rest
On the snowy pillow's breast,
As sinks the day-king in the west
Upon some pearly cloudlet's crest.

Whispered silence in the room,
Solitude as of the tomb,
Darkness that's akin to gloom.

Childish voices mute and still,
Hushed by sleep, as mountain-rill
Bound in ice-bands, bright but chill.

Children slumbering, free from dread,
Mother praying by their bed,
Angels watching overhead.

Evening's solemn silver chime,
Like some fairy's magic rhyme,
Meting out the flight of time.

And a Father's eye above,
Viewing all with look of love.

RELICS.

IN the dusty drawer of an old bureau
Lie those faded things of the long ago ;
There are locks of gray, that hoar heads did wear,
And delicate ringlets of wavy hair ;

There's a silken curl from an infant's head.
And tresses of gold o'er which tears were shed,
And down in a corner, preserved with care,
Is a precious morsel of silver hair.

They are folded fondly, and wrapped up well.
In paper whose feeble pencilings tell,
How love's hands gathered, and hoarded there.
Those varied tresses of treasured hair.

This dark-brown fragment was wont to rest
On the brow of a mother benign and blest,
'Twas reverently shorn from her forehead fair
By a daughter whose tears dimmed the dead one's hair.

This sun-tinted ringlet was sadly shed
From the beauteous brow of a baby dead,
Whose mother knew it had gone to share
The home of her of the dark-brown hair.

The auburn, the silver, the gold, the gray,
The bright brows that bore them have passed away,
They are lying low, crowned by dewdrops rare,
And a fond heart weeps o'er those locks of hair.

They are all she has of the loved ones now,
And hand will tremble, and head will bow,
For the dusty drawer in the old bureau
Holds all that is left of the long ago.

THE pretty yellow crocuses were sleeping in their
    beds,
The winter frost still curtain'd in their little fragile
    heads,
Not e'en a soft wind whisperéd a word about the spring.
When she came in her sweet beauty, a tiny helpless
    thing.

Her mild eyes opened, wondering at all she saw and
    heard,
And she nestled on my arm like a piping half-fledged
    bird,
Dear gentle human blossom ! how I blessed the
    cherub band
Who gave her from their number in yon fair celestial
    land.

As day by day went gliding past she all more lovely
    grew,
Her soul caught up new fancies, as daisies treasure dew.

She held them in her bosom, but she flashed them
from her eyes,
And she filled the house with sunshine and prattlings
wondrous wise.

Still, like a little fairy thing, she wanders out and in,
And seems as if she ne'er could feel the weight of
care or sin ;
Oh ! may my darling ever wear her childhood's stainless guise,
Which marks her one whose spirit holds close converse with the skies.

TRYING HIS WINGS.

WITH an eager light in his bright blue eye,
And a fair brow lifted, untamed and high,
With feet that fleet as the wild doe springs,
My first fair fledgling unfolds his wings.

He has cast aside every childish toy,
With the careless pride of a happy boy,
And over his shoulder a gun he swings,
My birdie bright, with the untried wings.

He turns away, with a glad disdain,
From the woman-love that would still enchain,
And my woman-fears he for ever flings
Far, far away, from those opening wings.

Impatient to walk on man's daring way,
What now to him is his sister's play?
How weak and small seem those little things,
So loved *before* he had dreamt of wings.

II

They cannot bear him far, far or long,
Those new-found pinions, they are not strong ;
But gaily his young heart bounding sings
Of coming joy that must have no wings.

So, gladly and fearless my bright bird tries
From childhood and childhood's dreams to rise ;
I joy that his love to the old nest clings,
While fluttering thus fly his half-fledged wings.

A DREAM OF OTHER DAYS.

OH ! I have had a dream of other days,
When on me shone your watchful kindly gaze,
When naught on earth could such pure light supply.
As that which on me fell from your fond eye.

I was your nursling then ; your tender arm
Was ever stretched to guard and guide from harm :
My baby-forehead nestled on your breast,
The place in all the world I loved the best.

Oh ! I have had a dream of other days,
When household lights fell on a fading face,
When sad eyes told of suffering, sore and long,
Yet merry laughter spoke a spirit strong.

I stood beside you then.   I, too, was changed,
My heart from its *one* idol far had ranged ;
But still, O still ! how could it other be ?
You were my guardian angel on life's sea.

Oh! I have had a dream of other days,
Of when your side became my constant place;
A few short years, that found us ever still
Companions close, thro' paths of good and ill.

They said that then they scarcely could divine
Between your gentle face and voice and *mine*—
So much alike.   It was not strange, though true,
That I had borrowed even your features' hue.

Oh! I have had a dream of other days,
When, groping darkly through a cloudy maze,
I found your hand that led me still aright,
Until I walked once more 'mid sunny light.

Your task was done.   Your wayward nursling flown,
And round your feet have *other* flowerets grown;
My path is far across a widening main,
'Mid anxious hopes and joys, and grief and pain.

But oh! that dream, that dream of other days,
It calls me for a space to thought's byeways;
It bids a memory wake that half had slept—
A memory by whose cell some hopes had wept.

My sister, my loved sister! can it be
That thus time's waves have parted you and me?

Oh ! have the ties, that bound so close and fast,
Unloosed and widened thus so far at last ?

Nay, nay; not so. That dream of other days
Will keep alight love's bright unflickering rays ;
And you and I, though journeying far apart,
Are sisters, friends, companions, yet in heart.

The golden chains of childhood, youth, and home,
Are round us wheresoe'er we heedless roam ;
We *cannot* loose those bands, they hold us still,
And rivet thought and love beyond our will.

TO "LITTLE HARRY" ON HIS BIRTHDAY.

WHAT can thy thankful mother say,
    Whose blessings have been rare?
How can her heart speak out this day,
    Save with the voice of prayer?

Through years of buffeting and strife
    My God has watched o'er me,
And what was one weak, worthless life
    That it so cared should be?

And oh! the gifts that he hath showered
    Around my wayward feet,
So oft and rich my pathway flowered,
    That even grief was sweet.

But—blessing rarest, choicest, best—
    He gave *thee* to our care ;
No wonder then thy mother's breast
    Is filled to-day with prayer.

And day by day He's giving more,
    For every blissful year
Adds something to thy spirit's store,
    And gives us cause for cheer.

Well may our hearts brim o'er with love
    To Him, our gracious God,
Who sends such blessings from above,
    And spares the chastening rod.

Oh ! may our eyes aye turn from sin
    Towards the land of rest ;
May we Heaven's holy harbour win,
    And Him our Father blest !

"AND THE NUN-BUOY TOLLED A
KNELL."

HE was gently laid on the lower deck,
　　As the evening softly fell ;
And the proud old flag of our country wrapped,
　　The form that we loved so well ;
And the crew slept peacefully—naught for him
　　Save " the nun-buoy tolled a knell."

Oh ! tell you me so ?　And did no eye weep
　　For him in his manhood's prime ;
Did they slumber on, though they knew that he
　　Had bidden farewell to time,
That morning would see their companion laid
　　'Neath the sod of a foreign clime ?

Was there no heart sad ?　O yes, far away
　　In his own bright happy home,
A mother woke from her sleep that night,
　　With dreams of the crested foam,
And the ship that had sailed, with her best beloved,
　　Round the great wide world to roam.

She awoke; for alas! that dream so dark
   Depicted a sea-rocked bier,
And the wavy hair that she knew so well,
   Falling over the brow severe,
Where sat enthroned in his awful state,
   King Death robed in mantle drear.

She woke from her sleep, and the vision fled,
   But where is he who can tell,
If *alone*, for the hope of so many hearts,
   The anchor-buoy tolled a knell?
Perchance the mother, in sleep, was near
   The ship on the tidal swell;

Perchance she was there, and in spirit bowed
   O'er the form of her noble child;
Perchance she had fondled the palid brow.
   And the lip that still sweetly smiled;
For surely *something* was there, to bewail
   One struck by a death so wild.

O yes, surely yes! And the same old sea
   That girdled the island lone,
Where his youth had passed like a joyous dream.
   Sang low in a saddened tone,
A requiem weird for the bright young dead,
   And the north wind harped a moan.

When the stranger band laid him down to rest,
   A stranger in strangers' land;
The ocean rolled up to his lonely grave,
   With a sound of his island strand.
It held on its billowy breast the tears
   And sighs from his kindred borne,
And it sang the dirge of the noble dead,
   From life's fairest promise torn.

The wild waves wailed for our darling one,
   And, brought on the night-wind's swell,
Came a mother's spirit, by anguish rent,
   To weep by that distant dell,
So something besides the lone anchor-buoy
   For our brother breathed a knell.

BELLA'S BIRTHDAY.

I CANNOT give some golden gift
   To mark thy natal day,
I cannot bid dear music's voice
   Awake with some fond lay,
I cannot, in thy listening ear,
   Tell what my heart would say ;

I cannot, from yon bending boughs
   Their autumn verdure tear,
And weave a wreath of varied hues
   For thy bright brow to wear,   .
I cannot place sweet summer's last
   Fair flowers amid thy hair ;

I cannot, oh ! I cannot, kiss,
   The gentle lips I love,
Nor hear them speak, nor see the smiles
   That round their portals rove,
As light-robed forms, who throng to grace,
   Yon star-clad realm above.

I cannot give, though fondly fain,
    My own, my sister-share
Of tender greeting, only *this*,
    A heart-felt, heart-sent prayer,
That God may guard and guide thee still,
    And make thee aye His care.

And if beneath His sheltering wing,
    Safe, safe indeed thou art,
And nothing more is left to wish,
    Save what a longing heart
Whispers me *yet*, and bids me pray—
    Ne'er from thy side to part.

LOVE'S CORONET.

LOVE made a golden coronet,
  And wove a golden chain ;
On youthful brows he placed the crown,
  Round loving hearts the rein.
There were bright gems of matchless worth
  Set in that flashing zone,
Whose jewel-rays lit the twining links,
  As love had lit each stone.

A little pearl, of lambent light,
  Was missed one weary morn,
'Twas said a spoiler's hand had ta'en
  What they had proudly worn ;
Their crown of love had rarer gems,
  And yet their loss was pain,
For precious was the tiny pearl,
  And broken was the chain.

Yet flashed the glowing coronet
  Back to the light of day,

While darkly hid away, 'twas thought,
　The missing jewel lay.
Love wondered where his gift was gone,
　And turned with anxious gaze
To mourn beside the shattered links,
　And wake their clouded rays.

Love's fingers filled the vacant place
　With love's own gracious gold;
But a bright and blue-eyed amethyst
　Fell from its circlet cold;
'Mid gloom and night they sought it long,
　Love wooed it back in vain;
And low along the murky earth
　Was dragged the lustrous chain.

While love yet wept that jewel lost,
　A ruby, richly rare,
Was plucked in haste, and rudely borne
　Beyond their ken or care.
Love bound his golden coronet
　More closely round each brow,
And gave more gems, whose weary weight
　Made aching heads to bow.

Love gathered up the lone links left,
　And strove to wind them fast;

But hands *more* strong yet held the chain.
  And scattered to the blast
The gems that still so gladly gleamed
  Among the glittering gold;
The rarest jewel of all was ta'en,
  Though fain their hearts to hold.

Love, sadly wondering, wended far
  To fairer realms away,
What saw he *there*, to wake once more
  His wistful eye's bright ray?
He saw upon a kingly brow
  His radiant ruby set,
And the pearl and amethyst nestling warm
  On a loving and kingly breast.

Love saw a band of dazzling light
  Around that royal One,
And *there*, " the richest gem of all,"
  Shone clearer than the sun.
Love gazed with burning awe and joy.
  For, twined by angel's hand,
He found the missing broken links
  Ta'en from his golden band.

Not lost—not ta'en—not broken now.
  Love's jewels, love's golden 'chain,

And with a gladdened heart and smile
   Love turned to earth again.

Love made *more* golden coronets,
   And from that same fair crown
He borrowed jewels to set anew,
   And, smiling softly down,
He whispered, " You shall find your gems—
   Lost, some with joy or pain ;
And up in heaven you'll find unbroke
   Love's earth-wrought golden chain."

BABY-DREAMS.

HUSH, hush ! for my baby has gone to rest.
And angels keep guard by the little nest ;
They whisper sweet things in those infant ears,
And the boy smiles out at the sounds he hears.
Hush, hush !

Hush, hush ! for his slumbers are gilded bright
By heavenly dreams that beguile the night ;
Those angels that watch by my baby's bed,
In golden fetters his spirit have led.
Hush, hush !

Hush, hush ! they are whispering of calm bright skies,
That match in their hue with the boy's glad eyes ;
They tell him of breezes as light and free
As spirits that float on those soft winds be.
Hush, hush !

Hush, hush ! for they tell of their heavenly home,
Of the fields above, where they love to roam ;
Of the flowers that bloom and can never die,
Of saints who rejoice through eternity.
Hush, hush !

I

Hush, hush! they are tuning their harps of gold,
To sing of the lambs of the Saviour's fold;
Of the little babes that have spread their wings,
And opened their eyes by immortal springs.

Hush, hush!

Hush, hush! they are telling of Jesus' love;
They would cull my flower for the fields above,
They would lure my boy from each earthly snare,
And give him to Jesus to love and care.

Hush, hush!

Hush, hush! for those angels still watch the while,
And the boy yet slumbers, and sweet the smile
That shines on his lip, and his half-closed eye,
Telling of watchers, unseen, though nigh.

Hush, hush!

Yea, hush! let him smile, let his dreams be sweet,
Such converse with his pure spirit is meet,
To hearts, that are dimmed by the world and sin,
Such visions of bless may not enter in;
But an infant's soul is as free from taint
As an angel spirit, or ransomed saint.
Then slumber, my babe, may thy dreams be sweet,
Such converse with thy pure spirit is meet.

Hush, hush!

THE TWO MAGGIES.

WE had a sweet sister when we were young.
Her ringlets of gold to her fair neck clung,
And as pure a soul through her blue eyes smiled,
As ever abode in an earth-born child.

She lingered on earth but a little time,
She left us soon for a happier clime ;
Her place was vacant, her spirit was gone,
And her form was laid in the churchyard lone.

Long years have gone past ; to our brother's side
There has come a young and a gentle bride,
Her soft eyes are dark, but she bears *the name*
Our sister in heaven was wont to claim.

Oh, she bears the name of that sister fair,
Who went long ago to our Father's care ;
And I fain would think, He has given again
The darling lost, amid sorrow and pain.

THE SAINTLY RAIMENT.

"When little Harry go to Heaven, then little Harry get on nice clean pinafore, and new shoes and socks."

FAIRER far than earth-made garment,
    Purer robes thy form will wear,
When, a thing of sinless beauty,
    Thou art wafted through the air ;
Not e'en mother's hand may fashion
    Garb befitting for thee *there*.

When thy free glad spirit mounteth
    To the land of blissful rest,
Not a mother's hand will robe thee,
    Not in mortal clothing drest ;
God will give a spotless raiment
    That will deck my darling best.

Clean and new, and pure and perfect,
    Will that heavenly mantle be ;
Jesus bought it by his suffering,
    Washed it in His blood for thee,

Far more fair than those *I* fashion,
  Far more bright than aught *I* see.

But though I can only, darling,
  Clothe thee in an earthly guise,
I can lead thy fancy upward,
  I can teach thy soul to rise,
I can bid thy hopes to anchor
  Where the land of promise lies.

And if all I hope and pray for
  Comes to bless thy pathway fair,
Holy will thy life on earth be,
  With no " ceaseless, cankering care ;"
And at last, when mounting heavenward,
  Thou the saintly garb wilt wear.

DEAR sister, when I see you place my baby on
    your knee,
The days gone by, almost forgot, unveil themselves to
    me ;
The clouds that Time, with stealthy hand, o'er
    memory's halls had hung,
Dissolve, and leave before my view the days when we
    were young.

And you have not forgot the past—the kindly tender
    past,
With all that childish happiness which went from us
    so fast ;
You still remember, sister mine, how merrily we played
From sunny morning's earliest blush till evening's latest
    shade.

And when my feet began to try to cross the parlour
    floor,
It was your hand that safely led the little trav'ller o'er ;

You were a tiny toddler then, just opening life's first
   page,
Yet guard and guide you were to me in earliest infant
   age.

No thought had I you did not share, our feelings were
   the same ;
Together dreamed we, wept and smiled. till earnest
   girlhood came ;
And then our hands unclasped their hold, for distant.
   though not lone,
Lay separate paths that henceforth fate had meted for
   each one.

Amid the stormy winds of life that gathered round me
   fast,
My heart could scarcely hear the voice that echoed
   of the past ;
For many years had swept along, and each eventful
   wave
Had borne me further from your side and nearer to
   the grave;

But now, my sister, when you place my baby on your
   knee,
The past arises in my heart, and whispers unto me ;

In gentle tones, distinct and clear, it speaks of those
    young days,
When by your side, and in your heart, I held the first
    fond place.

Sister, I can but thank you now for all your love and
    care,
And that your future may be blest will be my constant
    prayer :
Give to my little ones one-half of what you gave to
    me,
When you and I were children small as baby on your
    knee.

DEAR DAISY DAUGHTER.

A GARDEN of sweets is my baby-girl,
My island daughter, my orient pearl,
Borne from the skies on some cloudlet's curl.

And she is so fair, 'tis my greatest treat
To gaze on her face that's so wondrous sweet,
And where smiles of love gather fond and fleet.

The violet peeps out from her deep dark eyes,
The lily has shed on her brow its dyes,
And her mouth with a ruddy rosebud vies.

On her dimpled cheek the peach-blossom glows,
As silvery brooklets her laughter flows,
Her voice sounds like doves at the twilight's close.

Her delicate fingers in ours entwine
With the gentle grace of a clinging vine,
Her look is angelic when meeting mine.

She enters one's heart like the sun's glad rays,
She sheds bright beauty wherever she strays,
She commands all love with her winning ways.

The spirit that lives in my tender child,
Was sure from a cherub by her beguiled,
So loving it is, and so pure and mild.

My beautiful darling, my daughter dear,
'Twas a joyous day when you first came here,
God keep you to mother for many a year.

OUR BROTHER.

HE sleeps not where his kindred lie,
Beneath their native island's sky;
His youthful form was never laid
Within the churchyard's solemn shade;
No look of love bent o'er his grave
When it was dug beside the wave;
No lowly violet nestles near,
No dewy snowdrop sheds a tear;
Above his head there waves no yew,
No flower or thing his childhood knew.
'Twas stranger hands that laid to rest
The darling of the parent-nest,
The noblest branch that flourished free
Upon the old ancestral tree.
Beside the fretted rocky strand,
Which girdles round his Fatherland,
His childhood blossomed into youth,
Whose fruit was virtue, love, and truth;
And on his young and manly brow
Genius had wreathed her fairest bough.

But manhood came—and then he died,
The hope of home, its joy and pride.
What though the reaper's deadly dart
Struck at a mother's bleeding heart,
   And left a lasting sore?
What though a father's dreams of fame,
For him, the boy who bore his name,
   Were blighted to the core?
And what though many a tender friend
Wept his untimely early end;
And science lost a cherished son,
When died this highly-favoured one?
Death spares the sad, the weak, and old,
And takes the beautiful and bold;
And when *his* life was in its bloom,
Fate spoke that hard and hurried doom;
And then the hearts, bereft of light,
Could scarcely pierce beyond the night;
And aching eyes could dimly see
The hand which bent the stubborn knee
   That it might higher rise;
Who took the idol of such care,
That they might long to follow, where
The loved, the treasured, fond, and fair,
   Abide beyond the skies.

THE OLD GARDEN.

LET never a careless foot wander
 In the paths so dear to me ;
It was there where we played in childhood,
 Happy, and guileless, and free.

It was there our baby-steps pattered,
 Where our youth's light footprints trod ;
And some, who were with us at that time,
 Are lying under the sod.

'Twas our father's hands which once planted
 The trees that are bending now,
With their sheltering arms above me,
 And touching my upraised brow.

There is many a memory tender,
 Wrapped up in each leaflet's fold ;
The *leaves* they will fade, but the memories
 Will live till my heart is cold.

I remember now all the fancies
  That rose in my seething brain,
As I lay and looked through the branches,
  Towards the turbulent main.

I remember, I well remember, '
  The dreams and the dreamy walk,
And the beautiful summer mornings,
  And the evening's earnest talk.

It is hallowed ground, ah ! how hallowed :
  And I pray there may never come
A time when the cold-hearted stranger
  May dwell in mine ancient home.

VANISHED VISIONS.

BY the hearth, where flickering shadows
   From the deadened embers fall ;
By the hearth, where ghostly moonshine
   Steals along the darkened wall.

In the silence of the evening
   I bethink me of the dreams
That once gleamed as clear and hopeful
   As those shimmering silver beams.

They were quenched in utter blackness,
   And their dreary shadows lie
On the hearts they used to gladden,
   As stars a winter sky.

From the hearth the flames have faded,
   Chill and gloom are only there,
And the shadows from the hearthstone
   Brood where once the moonbeams *were*.

BABY ANNIE.

A LITTLE immortal blossom
   Has come to the island-nest,
To live in a mother's bosom
   To gladden a father's breast.

A little immortal being,
   A cherub sent from above ;
Earth-born, and yet all spotless,
   A precious token of love.

A little immortal spirit
   To train for the Fatherland ;
A tablet to mould and fashion
   With reverent heart and hand.

A little immortal baby,
   Of blessings the rarest, best ;
God's choicest gift to his children,
   And precious beyond the rest.

A little immortal daughter,
   A sunbeam to lighten home ;
A something to live and work for,
   A hope for the years that come.

TO BELLA.

THE sunny spots where long ago
We oft did wander to and fro ;
The tiny stream so wildly bright,
The garden old, our hearts' delight ;
The little flowerets blooming gay,
That blush to meet the smile of day ;
Our childhood's friends, our childhood's home,
Are all unchanged ; then, wherefore roam?

When we all meet at eventide
I think I see thee at my side ;
I miss thee in my evening walk,
And oh ! I miss our sister-talk ;
I look upon thy vacant chair,
And fancy oft will place thee there ;
But soon the vision fades away,
For far thy wandering feet do stray.

The summer time is coming nigh,
With long bright day and bright blue sky,

K

With happy hours, only too fleet,
With recollections fond and sweet ;
But, oh ! my sister, in those days
I'll miss thee from thy wonted place,
I'll miss thee from the household band :
Then turn thee to thy Fatherland.

TO A BROTHER.

THOU hast left thy native England,
   And the loving household band ;
They bid thee bring them treasures back,
   From that far foreign land.

The flowers that gentle nature
   Hath scattered richly there ;
The shells, the plants, the ocean gems,
   The beautiful and rare.

Birds that, like starry spirits,
   Float far on rainbow wings,
And like the saints of life and joy,
   Warble of heavenly things.

They say yon distant country
   Is lovely to the sight ;
They ask of thee to bring them back,
   Its treasures fair and bright.

Bring back with thee the tender,
   The honest heart and brave,
That now rejoiceth with the tide,
   That boundeth with each wave.

Bring back, bring back, the sunshine,
   That with thee did depart ;
Oh ! bring to us the love of old,
   The same untainted heart.

SAILING AWAY.

YOU'RE sailing out into a weary, wide expanse,
Of deeply rolling waves, whose white plumes dance
Beside the ship, as round our onward way
Through life the joys of earth about us play ;
And like yon dark and mighty sea, whose breast
Heaves blackly underneath that gay white crest,
So surge life's mighty cares in long unrest.

You're sailing out towards a long-wished goal,
With lightly-laden heart and sanguine soul ;
Your path across the main is gilded bright
With rays of hope, that chase all thoughts of night ;
On, on, she speeds, the trusty ship, and bears
A bosom filled with many pleasant cares.

The solemn evening hours are drawing on.
And underneath the trees I sit alone ;
An echo only comes to tell mine ear
That busy life's tumultuous strife is near ;

But, oh ! within a throbbing breast I hold
A thousand eager hopes and fears untold.

And swiftly to your side those winged thoughts fly,
And tearfully I lift a troubled eye,
And full of woe I utter oft the prayer
That heavenly love may make your path its care.
The shadows fall ; the sun sinks in the west,
The good ship passes o'er the ocean's breast.
God watch o'er you and bring *your* bark to rest.

THE SPIRIT OF HOME.

THE gloom of night is gathering round.
   A shade is on the hill,
The breathless wind wafts not a sound,
   And all the world is still.

Hark, hark ! was it some spirit's call
   That whispered in mine ear ?
" Though thou may'st wander far and wide,
   I ever shall be near.

" Around thee I will hover yet,
   To cheer life's darkling way ;
And like some guardian spirit kind,
   Be with thee night and day.

" Then fearlessly go wander forth,
   For though thou far may'st roam,
One faithful friend will aye be nigh,
The gladdening star of memory,
   The spirit of thy home."

OUT IN QUEENSLAND.

AT last, at last, the carrier-bird
  Has crossed the troubled foam,
And brought me from the brave old land
  News of my father's home ;
Letters to her lone wandering boy,
  From native England come.

Under the shade of foreign trees,
  With tropic skies above,
With swelling heart and brimming eye,
  I read the lines that love
Has sent to me by the good ship ;
  The leaf brought by the dove.

They scarce can know, beloved ones,
  How welcome and how dear,
How precious to the toiler come
  The words that bid him cheer ;
Like messages that greet me now,
  And glad this forest drear.

This little bit of writing fine,
   Ah ! mother, well I knew,
You would not let the vessel leave
   Without a word from you.
God bless that heart so far away,
   And yet so fond and true.

And, father, yours those lines of hope,
   That bid me trust in fate ;
That tell me that the good will come,
   If I but look and wait;
That God did never succour send
   To trusting hearts *too late*.

Kind sisters, how your letters teem
   With fancies sweet and pure ;
Ye gild my stony path with gold,
   Ye bid my faith endure,
Ye turn my thoughts to better things,
   To harbour safe and sure.

Brother ! in this small note of yours
   I clasp again your hand,
I see your face, I hear your voice,
   That bids me bravely stand
Up in the storm-tossed bark of life,
   And win its promised land ;

You tell me, too, of changes wrought
    In the old household band.

You say that to your heart has come
    A tender trusting bride,
And that our brother's soul hath now
    Another source of pride,
That children fair are growing up
    His Norland home beside.

With trembling hand, and eyes that fill
    Up with the rushing tears,
I fold and lay against my heart,
    To still its thousand fears,
Those records of the earnest love
    That bless'd my boyhood's years.

Those letters, like a fairy's wand,
    O'er every thought hold sway,
The misty forest fades from view,
    My lone life flees away.
I shut my eyes : I join again
    My brothers at their play.

The links that bind me to the past
    Are riveted each one ;

I feel my friends around me still,
   Though I am all alone.
The sea that disunites can bring
A soothing balm for every sting,
And every wave that meets the strand
Is a kind voice from Fatherland.

SHEDDED LEAVES FROM LIFE'S BOUGH.

THEY are falling, swift and silent,
　Falling like the autumn leaves ;
And the ghastly reaper binds them,
　Greedily, within his sheaves.

They are passing, ever passing,
　Like to shadows fleet and fast ;
And we dream we have them alway,
　And we wake to find them past.

They are going ever from us,
　One by one they fade away,
As the stars melt from our vision,
　When up wakes the king of day.

They are falling swift and silent,
　Falling into quiet graves;
Never more to heed the murmur
　Of time's many warring waves.

They are passing, ever passing,
   From earth's sunshine and earth's shower,
From the tumult and the turmoil,
   From life's leafy-laden bower.

They are going ever from us,
   Going to that land of rest,
Where our longing follows after,
   And we know that it is best.

A MOTHER'S WELCOME.

THY home is a peaceful one, free from all care,
And refuge from trouble is waiting thee there ;
My poor tired darling ! why, why, wilt thou roam ?
From the world and its bitterness come, come, come.

Pale sorrow has found thee, and sad was thy lot,
And that world had not for thee one peaceful spot ;
Thou'rt gloomy and lonely away from thy home,
Oh ! wander no longer, but come, come, come.

And didst thou then fancy that aught could remove
My care from an object that once was my love ;
Nay, though from my arms thou may'st ever still roam.
For thee in my heart there will aye be a home.

In thy mother's fond breast no anger could be ;
If erring, she only could mourn over thee ;
Yes ! even had sin stained that innocent brow,
My heart would have welcomed thee ever as now.

Then hasten, my darling, and never depart
Again from thy own mother's fond faithful heart ;
Alone on life's path thou must ne'er again roam.
From the world and its bitterness come, come, come.

A HEAVEN-SENT MESSENGER.

THERE was a sound of warring surge,
  Of thunder-voices raised and high ;
There was a wild wind's dismal dirge,
  A dark and clouded sky.

A low thatched cot beside the mere,
  A young head on a father's breast,
A sobbing cry of mourners near,
  A dying heart at rest.

Upon that faithful arm she leant,
  And smiled with every laboured breath ;
While love its supplication sent,
  To end the fight with death.

The fitful breezes swept the shore,
  And as they stole within the room,
A child of hope, they gently bore
  Where all was grief and gloom.

Through open casement came the breeze,
  With murmuring voice and quivering wing,

And *this* that o'er tempestuous seas
  Had come—a radiant thing.

A visitant of life and light,
  That dying eyes and watchers see,
A thing of grace—the emblem bright
  Of Immortality.

Soft-fluttering o'er the drooping head,
  And near the swiftly paling face,
And round about the humble bed,
  Before each wondering gaze.

Soft-fluttering came that glorious form,
  Soft-fluttering came that creature rare ;
In rainbow robes that mocked the storm—
  Such as the angels wear.

Soft-fluttering came the wingéd fly,
  And they, whose eyes had never seen
That offspring of the southern skies,
  Born of the meadows green,

Said God had sent to call the maid,
  Had sent from heaven a herald mild ;
And parents on the pillow laid,
  What late had been their child.

MY LITTLE COMFORTER.

LITTLE birdie, gentle birdie,
  How I love thy lay,
Cheering fancies sad and gloomy,
  Chasing grief away.

When a thousand cares and sorrows
  O'er my spirit stole,
That sweet note of thine so kindly,
  Did despair control.

When no dear beloved was near me,
  None to sympathise,
I would come and gather comfort
  From thy wondrous eyes.

Oh! they used to gaze upon me,
  As if fain to know,
Why, in such a world of beauty,
  Bitter tears could flow.

                    I.

From among the glossy leaflets
  I would see thee peep;
Timidly, and yet confiding,
  There thy watch thou'd keep.

And thy little song so simple,
  Softly would'st thou **try**,
And if I would never heed thee,
  Closer would'st thou fly.

Closer, closer, and yet louder,
  From that little throat,
Burst the lay so sweetly cheering—
  Music every note.

"Cheer up, cheer up; oh ! aye cheer up,"
  Sang thou unto me;
Thanks for that rare song, dear birdie,
  Offer I to thee.

WHERE I WOULD BE.

WHERE the wild north-wester whistles,
   Dirge-like o'er the lea ;
Where my native Isle lies dreaming,
   On its parent sea ;
Where the wintry winds are raging ;
   There I fain would be.

Where the solitary plover
   Calleth mournfully ;
Where his mate in plaintive love-notes
   Answereth tenderly ;
Where the surges wash the pebbles ;
   There I fain would be.

Where a dear home-circle nightly
   Join in sportive glee ;
Where a father, sisters, brothers,
   Meet and talk of me ;
Where my mother and my home are ;
   There I fain would be.

"THANK GOD FOR ENGLAND."

IN the midst of a sandy desert,
  Where never a rain-drop fell,
There flourished a lone oasis,
  With its buds and blossoms pale ;
And palms that waved o'er the herbage,
  As flutters a maiden's veil.

There a fountain of limpid water
  Flowed fresh by a shady grot ;
There the antelope sought a shelter,
  When the sun was scorching hot ;
While the thirsty and wearied traveller
  Thanked God for that verdant spot.

———

On the maddened and angry ocean
  There struggled a ship in vain,
For around her the darkness brooded,
  And the loud-voiced wind and rain ;
And no beacon was there to guide her,
  As she quivered like one in pain.

Then the sailor looked sadly upward,
  Where elements were at war,
And his spirit once more was gladdened,
  For he saw in the north afar
The light that he loved ; and, aloud, he
  Thanked God for the Polar star.

'Mid the brand and the blood of battle,
  By a sultry southern fen,
There fought for their country's freedom
  A band of heroic men,
Pressed sore by the foe, and numbering
  But one to the other's ten.

When the struggle was well-nigh ended,
  As shaft from the bow will start,
There sprang from that bleeding remnant
  One keen as a polished dart.
He guided the vanquished to conquer,
  He acted the hero's part ;
While the souls that so late had trembled.
  Thanked God for that valiant heart.

'Mid the envy and strife of nations,
  'Mid storms upon other lands,

'Mid the waves of contending commerce,
   'Mid rending of filial bands,
'Mid the wailings from war and famine,
   Our England still firmly stands.

Like the *one* bright blooming oasis,
   God's gift to the desert wild ;
Like the star of hope when it glimmered
   Through clouds on the ocean's child ;
Like the lion-heart in the battle,
   Is " England our mother mild."

She reposes like some great bulwark,
   While the weak and the strong all say,
As they seek from her free calm spirit
   A counsel in many a fray,
" Thank God for that goodly presence,
   Thank God for Old England this day."

LITTLE CARES.

I AM weary to-night, and burdened
    With a thousand little things,
That press on my laden spirit,
    And shackle its outspread wings.

I am tired to-night, and downcast,
    For earth, and its trifling cares,
Obtrude on my thoughts for ever ;
    Even mingle with my prayers.

The down from the wild duck's pinion
    Floats up on the heavy sea,
While the great grey cliffs are shattered
    By surf beating ceaselessly.

So the surges of life's dark ocean
    Fret ever around my heart,
And their merciless lips, like snowflakes.
    Touch even its inmost part.

I could bear to go forth and mingle
　In the battle's fitful strife,
Like a proud ship among the breakers
　Fighting for fame and life.

As the brave bark rolls from her bosom,
　The cold and engulfing wave,
I could dash from a dauntless spirit
　The waters that round it rave.

But the striving mysterious ocean
　Rolls past me on either side,
And only those surges reach me,
　As they rise with the restless tide.

Oh ! I long to be " up and doing,"
　For it wears my soul away
Thus to silently stand and suffer
　The drizzling but drenching spray.

But something within me whispers,
　That she who can look and wait,
And rise o'er life's smallest troubles,
　With a spirit nerved by fate,
Is noble as she who conquers
　The grief that weighs sore and great.

And something there is that tells me,
  That a woman's life must flow
In a current of holy patience,
  Submissive in weal and woe.

I have seen, when a storm was raging,
  How the white and crested foam
Wreathed gaily, in angry pastime,
  The brow of a rocky dome.

'Tis thus that I pray my spirit
  May with meekness meet and bear
Those troubles so small that vex me,
  And load my bosom with care.
I would twine my burden about me,
  And make it a garland fair.

GOOD IN ALL.

OH ! say not that there e'er could be
   A heart so cold, a soul so lost,
But keeps not one child-memory free,
A sunny gleam on life's dark sea,
   By raging billows never tossed.

Far down, where no dark blot can come,
   There rests a ray of happy light,
Pure as a drop from seraph's eye,
And as yon star-bespangled sky,
   Calm, radiant, beautiful, and bright.

Yes ! in each heart, however seared
   By sin or sorrow's blighting breath,
However dark, however drear,
There is one spot, all fresh and clear,
   Surviving every storm till death.

TREASURES.

MY treasures are rare, says the miser old,
They are heaps of silver and heaps of gold,
And I keep them hid in an oaken box,
That has brazen staples and iron locks.

My treasures are rare, says the youthful maid,
They are hearts and hands at my fair feet laid,
And orient gems to bedeck my hair,
And beauty and youth that can conquer care.

My treasures are rare, says the man of fame,
The worship of earth, and a deathless name,
An arm and a soul that can battle fate,
And thoughts that but with a harp's strings mate.

My treasures are rare, says the foaming wave,
A pearly grot and a coral cave,
And the dead that sleep far down in the sea
'Mid shells and seaweeds and breakers free.

My treasures are rare, says the mother mild,
In my home there gambols *one* little child,
And my Father keeps up in Heaven for me
The children I used by my side to see.

GOING HOME.

"GOING home!" 'twas the lark's sweet parting hymn
To the fleecy clouds at the twilight dim,
With a thrilling song, but a drooping crest,
And weary pinions that longed for rest,
The minstrel turned from the silent sky,
And " going home!" was his joyous cry.

"Going home!" and the war-ship bent each mast,
And proudly dared every angry blast;
She cleft the waves, and her worn sail
Was spread to fetter the faithless gale;
She bore a tired but conquering throng,
And " going home!" was the sailors' song.

"Going home" to the dark wood's covert nigh,
And the hunted deer raised his mournful eye;
He bore in his bosom a shaft of death,
And blood flowed free with his bated breath;
But strength came back to each shaking limb
With the peaceful rest of the forest dim.

" Going home!" 'twas the wail of an aching heart
That had felt the touch of a deadly dart,
It had launched its hopes on the world's cold sea,
And the waves had beat on it ceaselessly ;
A battered bark, 'mid the seething foam,
That could find no rest but in going home.

" Going home," in the dawn of the brooding spring,
And the ice-winds woke, as the strong white wing
Of the proud swan passed thro' the listening air—
He sped to the north, for his home was there ;
And as clarion-call to the battle high,
" Going home !" was the bright bird's onward cry.

" Going home !" and there fell on the dying face
The tender light of a heaven-sent grace,
'Twas a farewell beam, and the spirit rose,
Pure, perfect, and free, from all earthly throes ;
And as rapt it went on its onward way,
" Going home !" was the soul's triumphant lay.

" Going home to the peace of the parent-nest,"
It is ever the cry of the bleeding breast,
Going home to the friends that have loved us best,
To the only shelter from earth's unrest.
Going home to the haven of hearts distrest,
Going home, home, home, to an Eden blest !

"TILL THE DAY BREAK, AND THE SHADOWS FLEE AWAY."

THEY have gone to rest in the churchyard old.
On the bosom of earth that we deem so cold;
To them 'tis a quiet and peaceful bed,
Where calmly reposes each weary head.

There sweetly still, till the glorious morn,
Sleep the mother pure and her fair first-born,
Till the shadows flee for ever away,
And the sun comes forth at the dawn of day.

He had traced a path for her trembling feet,
She followed fast, that they soon might meet;
And angels joyed, when the mother and child
Met in the home of their Saviour mild.

There dwell they, in perfect and endless joy,
The mother so fair, and her gentle boy;
There they sing, till the shadows shall flee away.
And death will die at the break of day.

THE SHEPHERD AND HIS FLOCK.

UP the steep and rocky mountain,
  Wends the shepherd on his way;
Calls upon his flock to follow,
  But they tremblingly delay;
For the misty heights are o'er them,
  And the path is mire and clay.

Sweetly on his lute the shepherd
  Pipes a strain the weak to wile;
Stretches out his hands to help them,
  Speaks all tenderly the while;
But the clouds drift o'er the mountain,
  And they cannot see his smile.

"Come, my children, come," he calleth,
  But the stones lie everywhere,
And the thorns and briars beset them,
  And the lion in his lair;
So they turn them to the valley,
  Though no shepherd waits them *there*.

He, upon the mountain's summit,
　　Calls unto them once again,
But they say " The path is dreary,
　　Full of danger, full of pain ;
Oh ! we cannot pierce the darkness,
　　And to scale the crags were vain."

See, the shepherd bends, and softly
　　Folds the lambs within his arm,
On his kind protecting bosom
　　Shielding them from every harm ;
" *Thus*," he says, " I'll woo my flock,
　　Over thorny path and rock."

Swiftly up the hill he mounteth,
　　With the lambs upon his breast ;
And the ewes no longer waver,
　　See no danger, seek no rest,
Till beside their young they nestle
　　On the verdant mountain's crest.

Mothers ! thus it is the Saviour
　　Takes the children of your love,
That your feet no more may wander,
　　That your hearts no more may rove,
That your hopes may turn and anchor
　　Where your young ones dwell above.

THE STEAMSHIP "LONDON"—Foundered.

WHY do you look so pale, mother, and why do
    you weep so sore?
Is it because we shall never behold the bright green
    meadows more?
Is it because they're affrighted, and the ship so rudely
    rolls?
Or weep you because the captain said, " Think but
    about your souls?"

The wind is howling so loudly, I scarcely can hear
    the prayer;
But this is not Sunday, mother, and why are they
    kneeling there?
Say, why is that strong man shaking, as if with some
    sudden fear?
And why are our sisters sobbing, and calling on God
    to hear?

Oh ! see how that father kisses the little one on his
    knee ;

His eyes are heavy with tear-drops, and surely he
    cannot see ;

He says that he does not mind it, he's willing enough
    to go,

But thought for the tender children causes his bitter
    woe.

And, mother, the dark-faced stranger, I thought so
    wicked and wild,

Is speaking to God as humbly as if he were but a
    child ;

And the lady who laughed and chatted, and sang the
    whole of the day,

She's reading the Holy Bible, and bidding the pastor
    pray.

Dear mother, I am not frightened, for your arm is
    round me still,

And father kissed me and told me it was the Al-
    mighty's will.

I know that whate'er *He* orders is certainly right and
    good,

So maybe we'll find the Father 'mid waters so wild
    and rude.

You are not vexed with me, mother? I wish I could
    go to sleep,
And gently, with you beside me, go down to that
    mighty deep;
And then I would ne'er awaken till I heard the
    angels sing,
And saw the beautiful kingdom of Jesus our Shepherd
    King.

I wonder what ails me, mother, it seemeth as if 'twere
    night,
And bed-time, and I were tired, yet long for the sunny
    light;
It seemeth so strange; they're bidding each other such
    sad farewells,
When all are going together to where the Creator
    dwells.

I wish we were back in England. I'm sure cousin
    Charley said
The same, as he looked so fondly upon Marion's
    downcast head;
She only smiled back upon him and nestled close to
    his side,
And said it was best no parting, and he whispered,
    " My own true bride !"

Now, hush ! mother, hush ! you're weeping : and the
mother's grief was still,
No wailing was heard, no murmur against the Almighty's will ;
Some hands held each other tighter, and arms were
more closely flung
Round bending forms, that still nearer the loved and
the loving clung.

All heavily rolled the surges, and swept o'er the fated
ship,
While bosoms grew cold and silent, and mute was
each pallid lip ;
One cry of despair and anguish rose high o'er the
roaring wave,
Then all was quenched by the ocean, and hid in a
yawning grave,
Only *one* wail.   Ah ! God heard it, then all was over
and still,
And the sea and the breezes thundered, " It was the
Almighty's_will."

TO SPRING.

*" A welcome, a gladsome welcome give
To the beautiful maiden spring."*

THOU'RT coming, oh! thou'rt coming, on thy free
and joyous wing,
With thy blithesome smile of sunshine, thou beautiful
bright spring ;
Thou'rt coming with thy blossoms, and thy lovely
laughing flowers,
With thy budding trees and birds, with thy golden-
gilded hours.

Thou art coming with a halo of sunbeams round thy
face,
And their light, from hill and valley, will soon the
darkness chase ;
While upon each ice-bound brooklet a glowing warmth
they'll shed,
And they'll call the sleeping snowdrops from out their
wintry bed.

There be teardrops on thine eyelid, for oh! thou
    lovest well
Those radiant skies beyond the sea where summer
    breezes dwell ;
But let those April showers and mist flee from thy
    face away,
For the sun in all his glory will come with " merry
    May."

He will follow thy fair foot-falls e'en to this Norland
    isle,
And his countenance will beam on thee with many a
    kindly smile.
Then don thy brightest garment, Spring; and in *his*
    melting rays,
Dissolve away thy teardrops, ere come the summer
    days.

We long to hear the flutter of thy eager joyous wing,
For harbinger of blessings rare art thou, sweet maiden
    spring ;
We know that thou wilt chase away all winter's gloomy
    night,
So we welcome thee to Northland, thou beautiful and
    bright.

THE SPIRIT-FLOWER.

(To Annie.)

AND you have asked of me to tell
   The story of the flower,
To hang around its fairy bell
   The thoughts of some calm hour ;
You bid me seek in fancy's cell
   For some poetic power,
Whose gentle tones will soothe you well
   When dreary memories lower.

Oh ! well I wot the muse's wand
   Can trace no truer line,
Than that which lives in memory's land,
   Writ by a touch divine ;
And well I know your bosom holds
   A recollection sweet,
And that those dainty floweret folds,
   Can whisper comfort meet.

Does not your stainless snowdrop tell
    Of that rare spring-tide flower,
Whose petals oped where angels dwell,
    And safe from sun and shower?
Its perfect beauty blooms above,
    In everlasting spring—
Its sunshine, God's own golden love—
    Its shade, a seraph's wing.

Does not the sapless blossom speak,
    Of one whose bright young life
Was plucked in haste, lay crushed and weak
    Below the spoiler's knife ;
Of him for whom a place was made
    Within his mother earth,
As, "full of hope," the plant is laid,
    To wait its April birth?

Does not the modest floweret bring
    A thought of her, whose care
Culled for your hand, the child of spring,
    That you her hope might share?
Her love had reared above his grave
    The flower so soft and fair,
And angels bade it brightly brave
The wintry wind and wailing wave,
    And wake to verdure *there*.

Oh ! strangely sweet the thrilling thought,
  That while all nature slept
In winter's chains, your lost one sought
  To soothe the hearts that wept ;
And from his home by heavenly streams.
  He sent his sister flowers,
And straight that mound so cherished teems,
  With buds from heavenly bowers.

Gaze on the pure, soft, stainless thing.
  'Twill tell your aching heart
A sweeter tale of endless spring,
  Than I can e'er impart.
Its beauty, silent yet will sing,
  Of faith, and hope, and love,
My muse but soars on earth-born wing,
  Your flower is from above.

FEED MY LAMBS.

TAKE thou the little children up, and when upon
    thy knee,
Fold them within thine arm, give them of what was
    given to thee.
Oh ! feed them with the bread of life, and from the
    heavenly springs,
And show them how to find a rest beneath their
    Saviour's wings.

Call thou the little children oft, and when they come
    to thee,
Repeat to them what Jesus did to set their spirits free ;
And tell them how He bade *them* come, and how He
    kindly said,
" Oh, suffer little children to their Saviour to be led."

Bring thou the little children oft to taste the banquet
    rare,
That God has given for *all*, and to the lambs a
    gracious share.

" Feed them," for it was Jesus spoke : obey His last
    command—
Feed them with wine and milk that flow from His all-
    bounteous hand.

Set thou the little children in the highest, holiest place.
Do not their angels evermore behold the Father's
    face ?
Did not the Lord of love and life call forth a humble
    child,
And said, " Of such the kingdom is," in accents grave
    and mild ?

Love thou the little children well, the Shepherd loves
    them best ;
He cares the weakly, but the lambs lie on His loving
    breast.
No dearer name He can bestow upon His faithful
    friends
Than " little ones "—they are of all the choicest gifts
    He sends.

Bear from the little children much, their hands may
    place a thorn,
Or touch some half-healed wound thy heart for many
    a day hath worn ;

But, for each hurt the children give a thousand per-
fumed flowers,
And gild with God's own golden light life's dismal
lengthy hours.

List to the little children's talk, they come direct from
Heaven,
And it may be their guileless words are by the Father
given;
For some all vital work on earth oft an unconscious
child
Will wake a chord that holiest hands could only make
more wild.

Bless thou the little children then!   For God's own
holy Son,
Thy Brother, Priest, Redeemer, He was once a little
one;
And nearer to the throne than all the sainted infants
stand,
Feed, feed the lambs, that they may grow fit for the
Fatherland.

TO THE MEMORY OF A PET PONY.

VAIN fools may laugh, and worldly scoffers sneer,
  To see me weep for thee, poor humble friend;
  Yet will I mourn, and suffer them to smile,
While to thy grateful love I give a tear.

Ah ! would among our human kind there were
  Many like thee, steadfast in good and ill,
  How much of sorrow would be soothed away;
Friends would be faithful, loving, and sincere.

Oh, no ! I never marked a vice in thee,
  And now that thou art gone, I mind me how
  That dark eye gladdened up at my approach,
And beamed such fondling gratitude on me.

Friend of my youth's young days, 'tis hard to know
  That thou hast left us quite, and that the chain,
  Which knit my childhood with the present time,
Is severed, with thy life, as with a blow.

And yet to me it seems so : what a throng
  Of varied thoughts thy memory conjures up !
  I see again the heather hills, the vales,
The summer sky, the flowers, the birds' first song.

I see thee bound with springing step to greet
  My joyous shout and eager outstretched hand,
  And gently bend thy graceful neck that we
Might pat thy head, and give thee guerdon sweet.

With thee in winter-time, so rude and wild,
  Have I not often traversed hill and vale,
  Braving the cold blasts of the chilly north,
And thou the sole guide of the wandering child ?

I've watched thy dark and humid eyelids fill,
  As if with tears, if an impatient word
  Was uttered, and my heart feels heavy now,
When I bethink me of some word of ill.

I marked thy proud neck droop its bonnie head,
  I saw thy large full eye turn glazed and dim ;
  At last even I could coax no answering look,
So then they told our humble friend was dead.

I know, I know that some there are who say,
  In a far world the poor dumb creatures who

Have shared our sorrows here will share our joy ;
Would I could think so, would that I but *knew*
    That I would see thee, my poor faithful friend,
As I have ever seen thee, fond and true.

WHAT THE WATERS WOULD TEACH.

" LITTLE brooklet gliding
On thy happy way,
And with light step dancing,
O'er the meadows gay ;
Wandering thro' the forest,
Dreaming 'neath the trees,
Whispering to the flowerets,
Laughing to the breeze ;
Murmuring things mysterious
In a silvery tone,
Oh ! what canst thou teach me,
Brooklet bright and lone ? "

" Something I can teach thee,
Wilt thou learn of me,
Lessons of contentment,
Whate'er life may be ?
Heed not tho' thy pathway
Oft be rough and drear,

Heed not though the sunbeams
    Do not aye shine clear ;
But, like me, oh ! kindly
    Wander on thy way,
Glad'ning all hearts round thee,
    With a joyous lay.

" River, noble river,
    Bounding in thy might,
Like some warrior restive
    For the coming fight ;
Rushing boldly onward
    To the distant sea,
While thy crested wavelets,
    Shout rejoicingly ;
And thy rough rude pathway,
    Well thou dost pursue:
River, strong, proud river,
Canst thou teach me too ?"

" Thou may'st learn from me,
    Of a mind and will,
Strong, and still enduring ;
    Eager to fulfil
All of its high mission,
    And to reach the goal

N

Of its hopes and wishes ;
O immortal soul !
Learn from me to boldly
Strive and persevere ;
And thus strongly, nobly,
Make thy pathway clear."

" Ocean, grand old ocean,
Heaving to the shore,
Like some great heart throbbing,
Ever—evermore ;
Rolling, bounding, flashing,
Like some living thing,
Whilst thy voice of thunder
On the air doth ring ;
Whispering, wailing, murmuring,
Like a wayward child,
Oh ! what can I learn
From thee, ocean wild ?"

" Learn how weak and paltry
Is man's feeble might,
And how vain and worthless
In his Maker's sight
Are those works he reareth,
With self-righteous hand.

Canst thou weigh his glory
  'Gainst a grain of sand?
Listen to the murmurs
  Of my voice; though stern,
'Tis a noble lesson
  Thou mayest from me learn."

SUNSET.

LORD ! at this holy sunset hour,
   This hour of nature's evening prayer,
I'll own thy gracious might and power,
   And thank Thee for thy love and care.

Thou who hast robed this earth in green,
   And decked it out in fairest dress,
Who knowest each bud and flower, I ween,
   Will surely thine own children bless.

Yon bird that, wearied, seeks its nest,
   Is seen and cared for, Lord, by Thee ;
Then, sure, my soul should feel at rest,
   For Thou art also watching me.

More blessings, Lord, I will not seek,
   Than those of which I'm now possessed.
For Thou beholdest strong and weak,
   And Thou wilt bless as seems thee best.

In nature's voice I'll take a part,
　With nature's psalms my tribute raise.
And humbled soul and grateful heart
　Shall offer up their song of praise.

Yea, Lord ! at this still solemn hour,
　I'll bend in gratitude to Thee,
And only ask when storm-clouds lower,
　That Thou wilt love and comfort me.

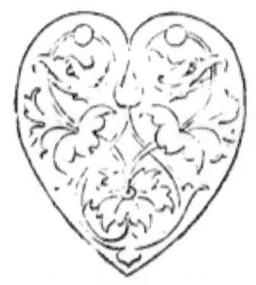

DREAMS.

'NEATH the shade of bending trees,
    Looking to the sky;
Listening to the summer breeze,
    As it passes by,
    Dreamily I lie.

Dreaming things, both strange and sweet,
    Of the time that's past,
Of the hopes, so vain and fleet,
    To the cold earth cast,
    Shivered by a blast.

Dreaming of the joys, the fears,
    All have shared with me;
Of the eyes bedimmed with tears,
    Of the smile of glee,
    Brightening life's lone sea.

Dreaming of a well-loved friend,
    Whose regard I thought
Never could have had an end.
    Ah! that love was naught
    But with bitters fraught.

Dreaming of a kindly heart.
    And a constant love,
That no storms could ever part,
    No rude hand could move,
    Nothing tempt to rove.

Just such flitting thoughts as these.
    Are the dreams that I
Dream, when, 'neath the wavy trees,
    Drowsily do lie,
Listening to the murmuring breeze
    As it wantons by.

KING CHRISTIAN'S MESSAGE TO DENMARK.

SOLDIERS of ancient Denmark !
   Gird on your fathers' sword,
The foes of mother country
   Have crossed the Eyder ford.
Stir up the Viking spirit,
   That thrills by mount and main ;
The cause of honour calls you,
   Let not it call in vain.

Maidens of ancient Denmark !
   Awake the patriot flame,
And bid the brave remember
   The race from whence they came.
Send forth your war-clad champions,
   Your smiles will make them bold ;
Go ! arm them for the combat,
   As did our maids of old.

Children of ancient Denmark !
    Pause in your artless glee ;
Read of your sires, whose sceptre
    Swayed over land and sea ;
Cast up to Heaven's great archway
    Each bright and earnest eye,
And bid your angel guardians
    Be where we fight and die.

Mothers of ancient Denmark !
    Lift up your hearts in prayer :
Commend your sons in battle
    To the All-Father's care.
Pray for the Danes undaunted,
    Who fight, and fighting fall ;
Pray for your soldier-sovereign,
    Pray for your warriors all.

Senate of ancient Denmark !
    Sons of a lordly line,
We fight for Danish liberty,
    For honour, right divine ;
We fight, as did the Viking,
    For the fame of Fatherland ;
We flinch not, though the foemen
    Strive on our either hand.

Denmark, dear ancient Denmark !
   For thee our hearts keep warm ;
'Tis thought of mother-country
   Which nerves each drooping arm.
'Tis memory of thy greatness,
   In former days of fight,
That strengthens for this conflict ;
   And God avenge the *right*.

RINGING OUT THE OLD YEAR.

TOLL the bell, toll the bell,
   In a low tone,
For hark ! 'tis the death-knell,
   The old year's gone ;
Shrouded in pure snow, mantled in soft
     snow,
Cold, old, and dying, he hurries to go.

Toll the bell, toll the bell,
   And the sad breeze
Whispers the passing knell
   To the old trees,
And ices the shroud of dreary white
     snow,
Where the old year lies forgotten and
     low.

Toll the bell, toll the bell ;
   Weep while you may.

Bid your hearts sing a knell
   Over the clay
Of those who were with you not long ago,
When the year that's dying was born 'mid snow.

THE END.